Also by Richard Sand

Fiction

Tunnel Runner
Private Justice
Hands of Vengeance
Watchman with a Hundred Eyes
Hell's Reunion

Non-Fiction

Protocol—The Complete Handbook of Diplomatic, Official, and Social Usage
Girard College—A Living History

For Professor David Webster

And thank you to Amy Salzman

"Blood will have blood."

—Macbeth

1

"Officer down! Officer down!" The distress call in the night. The universal call to arms. 1013. 1013. The plaintive cry for help. The alarm for all to set themselves aside and come rushing in. Tires squealing. Hearts pounding. Leaving your paperwork on the seat. Running with your holster so it did not flap. All of them like it was their brother down, their son, themselves.

And the sirens screaming, screaming. Making shrieking sounds, wailing sounds, chilling sounds. Keening cries for help and wailing for the dead. Rushing to the two with their gunshot wounds. The living and the dead. The white one, Lucas Rook, and the black one, dead Detective Graves. Like he had said, two Scottie dogs on a mirrored glass.

The naked girl had thrown the big silver gun off the roof. It picked up speed and hit the sidewalk like a falling safe. Then she ran inside where the swarming cops could not see her, because she was blind and because she had shot the one who'd shot her friend.

The black cops went to Dwight Graves first. Detective First Grade. Fancy dresser and looking a lot like Bill Cosby. And near him was Lucas Rook, bleeding out like his twin brother had a thousand years ago.

Captain Leonard made sure he looked like the commander of the scene instead of the political cunt, which was what he was. He knelt to get his photo snapped and then stood up for another and for all to see. Then he gave orders which might have been for lunch. "Now let's get this done," he said and was driven back to One Police Plaza to describe the opera that he was in.

The lobby and the elevators were filling up with cops and there was a helicopter overhead that was trying to set down. The tenants were irate that they couldn't go out to meet for drinks.

"Perhaps I shall withdraw my offer to buy," said the newly-weds who dreamed of a condo home.

"The streets opened up like a bitch in heat," said the ambulance driver, whose name was Orr. He checked his watch. "We made our time. Now let's get them in."

"GSW times two," he said at St. Vincent's door. "Mine's BP 40." He went into the hospital first.

"We gave them all we could," said the EMT, whose name was Fields. "Mine's DOA. He's the one who is a cop. The other was, I hear."

"It's upside down," said Orr. "It always is."

The EMTs gave up their spots when the doctors and the nurses came running up. An intake clerk with frosted hair came in with insurance forms.

"Shut your mouth," said Sergeant Flaherty on the scene. "The breathing one is Lucas Rook. Had his shield and twenty years before he left to do what he had to do. And the other one's a gold shield, Detective First Grade named Dwight Graves."

The sergeant turned to the doc, who had confirmed that Graves was dead. "You get me, too, Wally, what I'm saying here?" said Flaherty.

"I got you, Sarge," Dr. Buechner said. "Now let me do my job." He spoke to the crew coming around to work. "Multiple GSW to the chest. Let's see what we got." He took the curved laryngoscope with a right angle extension from the cart alongside the stretcher and passed the plastic tube between Rook's vocal cords and into his trachea.

A tall Asian girl cut off Rook's shirt and undershirt, then hung and ran a bag of saline. A resident collected blood in rubber-stopped tubes. Another injected morphine and succinylcholine into the IV.

"BP's dropping," said the nurse.

Dr. Buechner placed his left hand on Rook's chest, palpated the fourth and fifth ribs below the nipple, and cut a long incision directly into the chest cavity. He inserted the rib spreader to get inside. "Tamponade," he called and they handed him the tools to suction out the clots. As he cut through the dense pericardium around his patient's heart, its rhythmic beating started up again.

Buechner slid his finger under the left ventricle and turned Rook's heart. "What have we here?" he said. "Three-0 silk." He made a purse-string suture to close the hole and stepped back. "I love this job," he said.

The resident with red hair and freckles went lateral to Buechner's incision and made a one-inch incision of his own. He guided in a blunt hemostat and pushed a thick rigid tube in through the opening, then hooked the tube to the Pleur-evac and hung the first bag of blood.

"Good job," said Buechner. "Call upstairs and tell them we got one coming up."

Alfredo DiBona, M.D, was finishing up a valve and then came in. If anyone could fix a heart it was him. There were policemen outside Rook's door because the other cop was dead.

Lucas Rook floated out and back in broken parts. To the light and to the dark and to his twin brother Kirk, who had died in the street, shot down like a dog for who knows what.

Dr. DiBona had Rook in the operating room to do things right, and fixed the heart like he was repairing a watch to run for years. He got Lucas off the vent and then fought with Utilization and Review to keep him in the hospital for two extra days. "I spend half of my time fixing what's broken," he said. "And the other half seeing it's not broken again."

Sid Rosen came and sat with Lucas Rook. Joe Oren and Sam were there too. Jeanie stood outside and cried.

"Only relatives can stay the night," said the charge nurse, who was chewing gum.

"We're that," said Sidney Rosen, the garageman. "And more."

"That's right," said Oren, who ran the breakfast place where Rook ate like it was home.

"What are you doing here with these white folks?" the black cop who sat outside asked Sam as he came in. "He shot a brother down. Killed him dead."

"He's my brother in that bed, white or colored," said Sam. "And I don't know nothing about no other things."

The next day, Sid let in Valerie Moon, dressed up in the cashmere sweater and fancy boots Lucas had bought for her. She touched his hand and wept.

Catherine Wren came in last, his one true love, but the last to know. She held her hands in fists.

"This is wrong. It's wrong," she said. "You should be home with me instead of here. And there's police outside your door and you've been shot."

"It will all turn out," said Sid.

Rook's lips were parched and Catherine gave him some ice chips like Joe Oren said.

"What am I to do?" said Catherine Wren.

"Do?" asked Rosen.

"I mean what am I to do? Shall I stay? Shall my father get Lucas a lawyer? I heard them say downstairs another cop is dead." She got up and then sat down. "I don't know whether to stay or go."

"You can call is good," said Joe. "He won't like you seeing him with them tubes going in and out."

The nurse came and stood inside the door. "Two guest limit," she said.

"I'm going now," said Catherine Wren.

"Me too," said Joe. "I'll see to Jeanie. Then I'll be back."

Rosen picked up his book and started in to read. " 'He was an inch, perhaps two under six feet…' " He read *Lord Jim* for an hour or so and then put it down, telling Lucas that it was Joseph Conrad, not Robert who had the battery on his shoulder and was Pappy Boyington too and in the *Wild, Wild West.*

Two more hours passed, then Rook spoke the first since he went down. "Still here?" he said.

"To keep the *maleichamoves* away, Lucas boy, the Angel of Death."

Rook wet his lips. "He's coming here, Sid, he better not come alone."

2

There were cops all over the roof where Lucas Rook and Dwight Graves were shot. Two detectives knocked hard on the door where blind Grace Savoy lived.

"I was hiding under my beddy-bye," she said, coming out naked with a cigarette in her hand and one behind her ear.

"This piece of ass is showing off her snatch," said Detective Stanley Antopol, walking over to her. "Let's get some clothes on, lady," he told her.

Grace Savoy went back into her apartment with Detective Antopol and his partner, Joe Carillo, right behind her. "Too much noise," she said. "Like when I shot that feller dead."

"We met before, last year," Carillo said. "We're going to look around, okay?"

"When my doggie died. Thrown off this roof. I remember that."

"Where'd you put the gun, Ms. Savoy?" asked Antopol. "I can smell you just fired one."

"I shot him dead, you mean. You're Stan the Man. You were here too when my doggie died. He was bad when he went to the bathroom inside, but I never scolded him." She sat down on the brocade sofa and peed herself.

"You got this, Joey?" Antopol said. "I'll go tell the boss."

He went back outside and got Lieutenant Amodei, who was heading out to spin this cluster fuck.

"The naked chick, Grace Savoy, she just confessed, boss. We got this, right?" He reached for his smokes, but stopped.

"You got it, Detective. Now get her dressed and back to the house."

"She's crazy, boss."

"Maybe she is and maybe she's not. What are you telling me?"

"I think we should take her back, at least get her statement written up, but she's as crazy as a loon for sure and maybe she hangs herself or whatnot. She just peed herself. And we want to find the weapon, boss."

"We got what was left of it, Detective. She threw it off the roof."

"Then we're good to go, boss," said Antopol.

"Don't fuck this up more than it is," said the lieutenant. "We got cops shot up here. You get her dressed, she goes to St. Vincent's. You and Carillo get the arrest. Now let me do what I got to do."

Antopol was about to light his smoke when Carillo and the girl came out. "I'm blind as a bat, but I saw it all," she said. "Didn't I dress up nice?"

"Of course you did, dear," said Detective Antopol. "Now let's take a little ride, okay?"

"That too," she said. "Goobledygoo, goobledygoo. I shot him good."

Antopol and Carillo saw that she was transported and then called back to the 6th precinct to confirm the pinch was theirs.

"Good catch," said Carillo. "We could use it. Now let's grab some lunch before we're up to our asses in paperwork and people wanting our autographs."

"Anywhere take's Masterbadge is good, Joseph. I'm kind of tapped with this divorce thing. I'm giving her everything I got and she still wants more." He lit his smoke and took a deep drag. "She sucked my dick like she's sucking my blood, we'd still be together."

"Them smokes must be six bucks a pack, pardner, which is one of the main reasons I quit. How about we eat at my cousin's?"

"As long as I don't got to eat no sick shit like last time, duck fetuses or whatever," said Antopol.

"*Balut.* How about you stick with the *dinuguan.* Fix you right up."

"I don't even want to know, partner. Probably shark's nuts or the like."

"Blood pudding," said Carillo. "You'll love it."

The detectives handed the scene over to the ranking uniform, then headed out. Two geared-up woman cops from Emergency Services got in the elevator. "Hello, ladies," said the black one, whose name was Parks.

"Well if it isn't the cowboys," said Antopol. "You lasso any of the bad guys with them ropes?"

"We use them to 'repel,' " said Park's partner, a hard-looking white woman in her 30s. "You know, 'repel.' Like you've been sitting in a hot car in the summer sun and the closest you've gotten to deodorant is walking by it at the supermarket."

"Easy, girls," said Carillo.

"You wish," Parks told him. Then, "I knew Graves. He was a good cop."

"So was Rook, from what I hear," said Antopol.

"Internal Affairs' going to be all over this," said Carillo. "A cluster fuck is what it is."

"Graves was a good cop," said Parks again.

"Cluster fuck, I say," Antopol said. "That says it all."

"You boys get in trouble, we'll be there to pull you out," called Parks' partner as they mounted up.

Lots of bosses in the lobby and outside. Captain Leonard back for more pictures. Two strangers wearing lots of braid, and a fat man in civvies who had the "Deputy Commissioner who never spent a day in the street" look. Carillo and Antopol saluted. The pair from ESU gave it their best "rough and ready" look.

Carillo started to turn around, but Antopol held him up. "Let it go," he said.

"You think her partner ties her up and what not before they get their jungle fever on?"

"That is if she hasn't gone over to the dark side. I mean instead of the other dark side, Joey. If you know what I mean."

"I do, Stanley, I do. Now off to our island paradise, which we shall enjoy with several brightly colored drinks with little umbrellas in them."

Detective Carillo started up their unmarked and pulled away to Mercer Street for a lunch that reminded him of family and a chat-up of the waitress, who reminded him of his wife before the extra poundage and her moustache came on.

Pandan Island was decorated with pictures of the Minduro Philippines Resort and even a picture of the Marcos family. Mandy was decorated with new pregnancy.

The owner came up to see his cousin and brought them to a booth. "She won't even tell me whose it is, Joseph." He shook his head. "Such a sin and embarrassment." He took the menus away. "As I recall, your partner here is not so comfortable with our cuisine. Some *longanisa* and *bistek* then. A simple salad."

Antopol looked at Joey Carillo and nodded.

"And a Diet Coke," he said.

"And two rounds of drinks. The prettier the better," said Joey. "With little umbrellas for my friend."

"Of course, I'll serve you myself. My niece should stay where she is so that you cannot see her disgrace."

The drinks came and then the food. Carillo had his raw seafood in vinaigrette and *la patz batchoy*. The alcohol enabled Antopol to almost enjoy his meal.

Carillo's cousin served homemade flan and waved off the attempt to pay. "*Patawarin po ninyo ang aming mga pagkakakamali*," he said.

"*Hindi koalum kung papauno ko po kayo mapapa salamatan sa in yong kabutihan,*" Joey answered.

"What was all that?" Antopol said when they got outside.

"He said he was sorry, meaning embarrassed, and I said thank you for lunch and that you were the baby's father."

"You didn't," said Stanley.

"The question is did you, partner?"

"Not this one I didn't, Joseph. Not me. Not once."

They drove back to the precinct to make sure they were down as the Arresting on the Graves-Rook mess and then over to check on their suspect at St. Vincent's Hospital. She had been admitted and moved to the psych ward.

The two detectives joined the circus. Some residents going through the motions with Dwight Graves, who was still dead, and their boss making sure that all the paperwork read "Dead on Arrival" so it didn't add to the ER's mortality census. Grace Savoy had completed her emergency psych evaluation and was upstairs.

Carillo and Antopol went to the Behavioral Health floor.

"You two gold shields must be here to see our new patient," said the head nurse at the desk.

Stanley checked her nameplate while trying not to stare. "You recognize talent, Nurse Williams," he said, gesturing toward his detective badge.

"Me or you?" she said.

"Clever girl," said Carillo. He started down the hall.

"Hold on, Detective, I got a job to do," the nurse said. "And one of them's to see nobody gets past this desk's not supposed to."

"Official police business," said Stanley. "You don't want to be obstructing that."

"Obstructing? I don't think so. You want to talk to the patient, the best I can do is have you talk to Dr. Doyle."

"You run a tight ship," said Carillo.

"Just like my daddy at the 1-7."

"The Hammer? He ran that desk like he was captain of the ship before he went out. Where'd he go?" asked Antopol.

"Alaska. And all this bonding's not getting you anything except Dr. Doyle."

A tanned, good-looking woman came down the hall. "That's me," she said.

"We're investigating the double shooting involving your patient, Ms. Savoy."

"Gentlemen, you're welcome to attempt an interview for all it will do you."

"Why's that?" said Antopol.

"Two reasons, Detective. One is she is non-communicative and clinically hysterical. The other reason is I've given her enough Haldol to calm her down that you're probably not going to be getting through to her."

"You mind we take a look, Doc?"

"Not at all."

She led them down the hall.

"Hot bod," whispered Carillo.

"Very," said Antopol.

Grace Savoy was in restraints. Without make-up she looked as much like a tomboy as she did a model with her close-cropped hair. "Gobbledy-goo," she said. "My doggie-doo."

"Your what?" asked Detective Carillo.

"What about your dog, Miss Savoy? The one that Westsider threw off the roof last year."

"Dead, dead. Arf, arf."

"I got that, Joey, word for word," said Stan Antopol.

Doctor Doyle ushered the two detectives back into the hall. "I don't know when she'll be of any help. I get an idea, I'll call you."

"She told us on the way in that she could hear a pigeon fart a mile away," said Carillo.

"I can as well," said the doctor. "So thank you for appreciating my figure. Maybe tomorrow afternoon. Call first."

"Will do," said Detective Carillo. "Will you be here?"

"Unfortunately not. My husband's taking me on a cruise. Now if you'll excuse me, I have other patients to see."

Carillo and Antopol had a complex and detailed discussion on the way back to the 6th about who would be the better lay, the doctor, the patient, or the Filipino waitress before she got knocked up.

"Do some more paperwork before we see the boss," said Joey.

"Dot our t's and cross our i's confirming we read her rights before she chirped." Antopol chinked his smoke against the station house door.

"Right, right. Now let's write up what we got, that we got a tranqed out, half a freak model-type who admitted to killing Detective Dwight Graves. That should ease the percolating racial shit around here somewhat," said Carillo.

"Speaking of shit, you mind writing while I drop a deuce and a half behind your cousin's cuisine?"

"Use the can up in Anti-Crime, will ya, partner?"

Lieutenant Jaluski of Internal Affairs came into the squad. "Gentlemen," he said. "Let's chat." Detective Ament, who was with him, stayed a step back.

"Got to see a man about a pound of cheese," said Antopol, heading for the stairs.

"I can wait. One of our finer traits, patience," said the lieutenant. "You two fine detectives caught this job before Downtown called us in?"

"If you say so, Lieutenant," said Joey.

"You got anything for me, Carillo?" asked Detective Ament.

"Hitting the head when my partner gets back."

"We can wait," said Ament.

Antopol and Carillo met in the hall and had a two-minute rehearsal to make sure they didn't get themselves in the mix, which IAB would do if they had a half a chance. Then they gave their separate statements and went out for a cold one to toast what assholes Jaluski and Ament were.

3

Lucas Rook was in and out of consciousness. Three thuds and he was down. The pain came after the weight of a thousand pounds, and then his heart shutting down, the other half of the elephant standing on him. Stay calm. They'll come or not, but take me somewheres so I'm not dying here, bleeding out like my brother did.

He could wiggle his toes. Him and Kirk used to wiggle their toes on the beach at Coney Island. Then Rosen was there in a hospital room and Joe Oren came and Sam, the cook. He thought he heard Jeanie call, but she should not be there.

One of the nurses smelled like vanilla. A guy nurse smoked too much and Valerie Moon had great tits. Catherine was there wearing pearls and telling him he needed a shave. She's wearing two strands of pearls. And a wavy picture of blind Grace Savoy blowing away Detective Graves a minute too late.

"You strong enough to talk yet?" asked Frank Jaluski from Internal Affairs.

"I smell rodents," said Lucas Rook.

"My, how things turn out," said Detective Ament. "We're doing fine and you got all those tubes running into you."

Joe Oren came in slowly from the hall because of his back and all that sitting, but he was big.

"You'll have to leave," said the lieutenant. "This is official police business."

"In a pig's eye," said Joe. "I know what's going on."

14

The uniform who was sitting outside came in. "Everything alright in here?" he said.

Ament waved him off. "We got this," he said.

"Nothing to sweat here, Rook," said Jaluski. "A cop shoots somebody, I got to do my job."

"Sure," Lucas said. He took a deep breath, which made him wince, and pulled the cord for the nurse.

Nurse Williams came in. Detective Ament went over to keep her out. Joe Oren walked over to him.

"You don't want to do that," Ament said.

"Is everything alright here, Mr. Rook?" said the nurse.

"Doesn't feel right," said Lucas.

"Don't look right, either," said Joe Oren.

"Funny boy," said Ament. "Funny boy."

"You ain't baiting me," said Oren.

"And you're not agitating my patient, none of you. You all have to leave."

"Let's call this a day," said Jaluski. "We'll be back tomorrow, Mr. Rook. Meanwhile, I'll see about your visitations so you're not so agitated. Now, everyone have a nice day."

"Cheese-eating prick," said Lucas as he hit his morphine pump.

Lieutenant Jaluski and Detective Ament made their next stop in the hospital. When they got up to the psychiatric unit, they found that Grace Savoy was no longer in her room. An obese black man was trying to reach his erect penis with his restrained hands.

"Lovely," said the lieutenant. "Absolutely terrific."

"At least what they say isn't necessarily so. I mean about his thing," said Ament.

Jaluski let the comment pass and went to the nurses' station. The supervisor was an older woman with thinning hair pulled back.

"Can I help you?" she said.

"Grace Savoy?"

"Next floor up. She was moved this morning."

"Who authorized that?" the lieutenant asked.

"The room is secure. Your officer is still outside there. Now excuse me, I have patients to care for."

"And I'm running out of mine," said Jaluski.

There was a policewoman outside of Grace Savoy's room. She stood up when she saw Jaluski and Ament with their gold shields flapped from outside their pockets.

"The suspect's inside, Lieutenant. She has her lawyer with her. From what I can tell, he's blind too and she's still out of it."

"How long the liar, I mean lawyer been in there?" asked the detective.

"Since I started my shift," said the officer. "Will you sign my memo book, Lieutenant?"

Jaluski nodded to the detective, who did the signing, and they went into Grace Savoy's room. A blind man in a three-piece suit stood up.

"Russell Spritzer," he said with an "R." He handed over a business card with printing on one side, Braille on the other. "Counsel for Ms. Savoy."

"I see," said Ament.

"I get that quite a bit," said the lawyer. "You have any questions, my client is not competent to answer."

Grace produced a significant queef.

"Right on cue, Counselor," said the lieutenant. "We'll be back tomorrow."

"Now let's make another run at Rook before we go," he told Ament in the hall.

They went back to Rook's room. The drugs had Lucas in bad dreams.

Sid Rosen was coming out of the bathroom as IAB came into the room. Jaluski showed his gold.

"He's sound asleep," said Sid.

"The nurse told me you're Sid Rosen. Close friend of Rook here?"

"Both, you could say," said Sid.

"There was a robbery in your shop. Detective Graves worked that," said Ament.

"I guess he did." Rosen sat back down and picked up his book.

"We'll be reaching out to you," said Jaluski. "I'm a friend of his."

"Of course you're not," said Sid. "And I don't know a thing. You want to talk to me, you'll talk to my lawyer."

IAB left. "Now let's swing by the 6th," the lieutenant said when they got outside. "Maybe Carillo and Antopol are not out snoozing in their unmarked."

4

The desk sergeant at the precinct was a pale man with a large port-wine mark on the right side of his face. He pointed to the sign-in book.

"Do we have a problem here, Sergeant Gormley?" said Jaluski. "Last I checked, I'm a lieutenant and that trumps being a sergeant."

"No problem here," said Gormley. "I'm just doing my job."

"Which means busting our balls?" said Detective Ament.

"No it does not, Detective. It means doing my job. So if you will sign in please and present valid corresponding identification as verification, I will be happy to grant your unfettered access and wish you Godspeed as you complete what must be for you another long and challenging workday."

"And then you'll call upstairs and give whoever the word we're on our way."

Gormley shrugged his shoulders.

Ament signed them in and they went up the fire stairs two at a time as Sergeant Gormley made the call.

Detectives Carillo and Antopol wished that they had taken lost time or were capturing some z's under an overpass, but they were doing the next best thing, which was being out working a cake job. Get that closed and then chase the OT on the Graves shooting.

Pus bag Douglas Krassen was pulling the phony realtor scam, taking deposits on non-existent sublets. The two detectives were on their way to meet him outside of a brownstone six blocks away from the precinct house.

"This time I'm the manly man," said Carillo. "Last time when we were working that fruit loop bar job, I was the femme."

"I don't hold my smokes right, Joey, I mean Joseph. I tried, but I don't get it right."

"So don't smoke for a half hour, partner. I'm Roy Rogers on this job. You're Dale Evans."

Antopol took a deep breath. "I start throwing a nicotine fit, you just ignore me, right?"

Carillo nodded as Krassen came down the street looking like he owned it.

"You're just going to love this. The building, the light, the location," said the scammer.

"Location, location, location," said Carillo. "You could even walk to work, Stanley, instead of taking that filthy subway."

"Filthy, filthy. But I think the light is going to be all wrong."

"Let's just see," Krassen said. "I've got two other couples dying for the place. I'm supposed to pick up a check from the Rubensteins." He checked his watch. "But first come, first served."

"Naughty, naughty," said Antopol.

The super had rented Krassen a key to show them the apartment of his vacationing tenant. A dollar a minute, like the massage parlor charges, and another hundred for a happy ending if they write a check.

The place was nice. Two bedrooms, center hall, bath and a half. Detective Antopol fretted about the light and that the toilet flushed too loudly. Carillo comforted him. Krassen looked at his watch again and then tried a little charm.

"I may be wrong, but this is you. On the other hand, if I've got to take a cab to Murray Hill to pick up the deposit from the

Rubensteins, that's okay too. It's just that she was such a harpy. No taste whatsoever."

"I do love it," said Antopol.

"We need to talk," said Carillo. The two detectives went into the other room. "We'll take it," they said when they came back.

"Fabulous," said Krassen. "I need a deposit for $2,400 to hold it. Douglas Krassen, Agent."

Detective Antopol sighed and handed over the check. "And we'll take you too, jit bag." He flashed his shield. "You are busted, busted, busted, jerkwad."

"There must be some mistake," said Krassen.

"Location, location, Mr. Flim-flam Man. Let's see if we can't hook you up with a jail cell with a view."

"And lovely light," said Antopol as he lit his smoke.

Jeanie Oren came in to visit when her father told her that Lucas Rook had all the tubes out.

"I just couldn't, Uncle Lucas. All those machines attached to you."

"It's alright, Jeanie girl. They were just circulating things, you know, 'out goes the bad air, in goes the good air,' like whatcha-macallit."

"CPR."

"Right, Jeanie. I'm a little forgetful. They say that's normal."

"I'm attached to you," said Jeanie Oren. "I hope you won't forget that."

Lucas reached for the cup of ginger ale next to his bed, but the pain got him.

"I'll get it for you." Jeanie Oren started to cry.

"You alright, Jeanie girl?"

"I wish I was older."

"No you don't."

"Yes I do. I'm almost done college, you know."

There was a knock on the opened door. "Dr. DiBona will be stopping in shortly," said the nurse. "And there's two men to see you. One of them insisted I give you his card."

It was Felix Gavilan, Esq., shyster extraordinaire from Atlanta. The other one must be his fag boyfriend with the chromed-up piece in his shoulder holster.

"Sure, sure," Lucas told her.

Jeanie Oren got up to go.

"I'll bring you some fruit when I come tomorrow," she said. She leaned over and kissed him on the cheek. "And I'm not calling you my uncle anymore."

"I guess not," said Lucas Rook. "And I'll call you Jeanie, not Jeanie girl or Jean, if it's okay with your dad."

"It's okay," she said. "Jeanie it is."

She left, but returned. "Those two men," she said. "Cover up your face. Their cologne is terrible."

Attorney Felix Gavilan came into the room after Jeanie left. He looked exactly the same as when they had first met when Rook got the Alterstein job. Hair perfectly black, skin perfectly smooth. The GQ fashion plate, except for the cufflinks of the scales of justice in gold and diamonds and the Roly the size of a clock radio. Only the assistant was different. The old cold-eyed Latin boyfriend was replaced by a new one, as perfect-looking and slim as the last one and with the same weird combination of "I love it up my ass" and stone cold killer about him.

The new boy stood off to the side. Gavilan adjusted his shirt cuffs. "You don't look as bad as you might," he said.

"How charming, Felix. And you came all the way from Atlanta to see me."

"I'm here on other business. From Peachtree City, Lucas. You did receive my announcement." He gave his assistant a hard look.

"I did, Felix. And the calendars." The cologne made Rook sneeze, which made him wince.

"Call this visit business and personal, Lucas. I'd like to handle your litigation for you."

Rook took another sip of ginger ale. "What litigation is that, Counselor?"

"For your injuries, pain and suffering, wage loss, cosmetic disfigurement. We've got some deep pockets here, Lucas. The City, the State. New York has waived its sovereign immunity protection. New York Court of Claims Act Section 8. Also the Hotel St. Claire, its holding company. Sorry I can't help you with Dwight Graves personally, I'm conflicted out."

"Slow down, Counselor. Run this back as if you wanted me to understand what you're talking about."

"You have the right to proceed for monetary compensation against the City, the police department, the state of New York, and the real estate entities for such compensation as may be appropriate to put you in the position you would have been had this terrible event not befallen you."

"Won't do that, Felix, against the PD or whatever. You know better than that, no matter how you spin it."

"Then there's your building and the company that owns it. Actually, there's been a recent change of ownership. Failure to adequately protect its tenants and so on."

"Anything else, Felix?"

"I cannot handle your claim against Detective Graves as an individual. I can recommend a colleague, however, for that part of the litigation."

Rook adjusted his pillow. "You're tiring me out here, Felix, so let's skip to the fact of how you picked this up and that you'll be going after my neighbor too."

Gavilan adjusted his two-hundred-dollar tie. "Of course. And as you shall certainly learn, I've been retained by Detective Graves' sole surviving relative and next of kin, Florence Simmons of Atlanta."

"And you'll be suing the City, Grace Savoy, me?"

"Not you, Lucas. Even I couldn't craft that."

"No way I help you with the PD, the City or Grace Savoy. We *straight* on that?"

Gavilan ignored the insult. "The building then. We can fashion something that'll work. I'm a clever man."

"And well-dressed too, Counselor. Don't forget that."

"Of course not. I'll call you tomorrow and let's see where this goes. In the meantime, get your rest, Lucas Rook. You look awful."

5

Lucas is up and walking after Dr. DiBona's next visit and he sees that something is not right. There's still a cop outside his door, not to mention that it's always a black cop. Anybody who can do half -assed police work knows he's not a suspect, but a half-assed material witness since Graves shot him before he got what was coming to him from blind Gracey.

The shift change was giving each other some tribal handshake as Lucas came back down the hall from doing his five-minute marathon in elastic hose.

"Somebody score a touchdown?" said Rook.

"Heard you was a wise ass," said the new one.

"True, true, Officer Nicholson. A wise ass who doesn't eat his dessert."

Nicholson looked at the other cop, whose name was Jones. "I don't touch the stuff."

The bedside phone rang as Rook completed his gymnastics of sitting down. It was Wingy. "Sorry I didn't get to talk to you sooner, Rook. I was away in Hawaii. It would have been our ninth anniversary. You get my flowers?"

"Very tasteful."

"How's the mending going? I heard you took a couple in the chest. I says not to worry, he ain't got no heart anyways. You get out, I'll be there if you need me. Or while you're in."

"I'm good," said Rook.

Wingy Rosenzweig was a good guy and a master drug dealer, specializing in out-of-date prescription stuff. A good guy and a good source of business. A little freaky about the late Mrs. R., her picture painted over his bed so he could see her at night. Then again, she was a beauty before the cancer got her and a saint since he had a flipper for an arm.

Lucas counted out his pulse and multiplied by four. He was supposed to do it after his hall walk, but he also was supposed to be grabbing up a bad guy or banging Valerie Moon. At least, hitting the heavy bag and having a cold one afterward. Do them all at once, that was his dream.

A resident came in to check his incision and vitals.

"Am I alive?" asked Rook.

"Am I?" asked the doc as he charted the numbers. "You want anything before I go and enjoy my first sleep in twenty-six hours?"

"Not unless it's a tiny bowl of red jello squares."

"I hear you. You need anything in the next fifteen minutes, scream real loud. The cop at your door is napping and they got the music on at the nurses' station."

"I'm going to miss this," said Lucas.

Rook called around to let the world know he was back in circulation, although he knew it would be a while before he could be back working the street. Hugh Sirlin at SDA hadn't bothered to wait to replace him on the bone-smuggling job for his funeral home empire.

"I'm afraid that corporate felt the matter was time sensitive," he said.

"Right."

"We do want to maintain our relationship with you," Sirlin said. "But the continuity of this assignment requires that you turn over your work product to your successor, Mr. Rook."

"Have whoever call me at my office," Lucas said. He tried a little dig about MJ O'Reilly, who they had shitcanned. "Tell Ms. Reilly I said 'Yo,'" Rook said.

"Of course," said Mr. Sirlin. "A Mr. Baum of Integrated Services will be contacting you for your work product. Do recuperate. I'm sure we'll be doing business again."

The next call was equally bullshit. Everett Warden, who had called him on the Helen Maguire job, which kind of wound up getting him shot in the chest, said that there was a "penumbra of conflict," whatever that was. "I am appreciative of what you did for me in New York, Mr. Rook, so I will make some calls for you."

"I hope you will do that, Dick. I do." Which meant if it wasn't for me, your getting popped by the PD while sporting just your fancy socks for a teenage prostitute would still be kicking the shit out of your life.

Owls Miksis was glad that he was up and around and had something for him. Follow the cheating boyfriend for the fag accountant. Split the fee. Lucas said he'd get back to him tomorrow. Rook called Skenadji, who had sent him Mrs. Politte. The case with the Brothers of the Half Moon had turned out golden for everybody, including her fancy lawyers on Park Avenue who also gave him zero. Then he went down the line with the lawyers. At the end was Ryan, whose number was disconnected.

Lucas took a break from his business calls that were getting him nothing and got up to take a pee. Make doubly sure you shake before you tuck. Nothing like the smell of urine on your hospital gown to convince you that you're only a half step from the Policeman's Home. Maybe share a room with Ray Tuzio, who had taught him the streets and saved his life coming through the door with his riot gun, and now was sitting in la-la land.

The lady from the food service came into the room. Only thing better to stimulate the appetite than a fat woman with veiny arms and a hair net, was the skinless chicken and steamed carrots.

"I'm on the Carnegie Plan, dear," Lucas said. "Check and see they have any pastrami on rye."

She served her bounty without comment and wheeled the cart back outside.

Lucas took a deep breath and pretended the tasteless meal was something he would actually eat. The dessert was canned plums, which warranted being saved as a joke for Sid Rosen, who was going to be by in another half hour.

Rook put the bottom end of his bed up and fell asleep. When he awoke Sid was dozing in the guest chair.

"You alright, Sidney?" Rook asked.

"Good, Lucas boy. Looks like you got some of your color back. You doing what they tell you?"

"So I can get out of here. In fact, I'm due for my evening stroll after I drain my vein. Which reminds me, while I was out they actually cut these off by mistake." He handed over the plums.

"Looks like your circulation wasn't any too good anyway," said Sid.

Lucas lowered his bed and made it to the bathroom and back. "Going for my promenade, Mr. Rosen. Care to join me?"

"Not too fast, Lucas boy," said Rosen. "I'm only good for the dog walking pace."

"No problem." He took the little dish of fruit off the tray. "Going to ask the uniform outside if these are his."

"Nobody outside," said Sid.

"Probably out counting his illegitimate kids. Meanwhile, let's do this."

Rook and Sid Rosen made their way around the hall, Lucas leaning on the cane they gave him because he was weak and his bad leg seemed wobbly. They passed the rooms of families making small talk while Poppa crapped into a pan and the room where gypsies brought in their own food and paid the hospital bill in cash. Then the hot chick in 516 and a room with the door always closed that two priests visited.

Rook stopped at the nurse's station. The male nurse who smoked too much was reading the *Daily News*.

"How long since the officer been away from my door?" Rook asked him.

"I saw him leave about two hours ago."

Rook turned and went back to his room. "Something's up they pull the detail in the middle of the shift."

"Like in *The Godfather*, Lucas boy? They pull the guard off of Marlon Brando's room and Pacino moves him."

"Could be, Sidney. How about you get me out of here. I got claustrophobia, paranoia, and bad food."

"You sure about that, Lucas boy? Your health comes first."

"Which is why I've got to roll, Sidney. Not to mention they're charging ten grand a day."

"If you say so, Lucas boy. You can stay at my place like when you nursed me after I got tuned up. Except you got to agree anything seems out of whack with the way you're feeling, we're right back."

"Deal," said Rook. " 'Do Not Pass Go' or whatever. Let's go down the back stairway."

The steps, even going downstairs, were harder for Rook than he expected, and he had to stop twice and lean on Sid Rosen as they went to the big Cadillac Fleetwood parked in the hospital parking lot. Lucas stretched out on the back seat.

"I'm glad to be out of that fucking place one way or the other," he said.

"Walking upright's good, Lucas. It beats the alternatives."

When they got to a block from Rosen's, Lucas had Sid cut the lights and take the alley. Rosen pulled up to the corner. There was a cruiser parked on Sid's block.

"Just because I'm nuts, Sidney, doesn't mean I'm nuts."

"We could go out to my old lady's place," the garageman said.

"No need to trouble her. Let me make some calls." With Joe Oren, you had Jeanie to worry about. A couple of old cop friends would keep their mouths closed, and maybe Tom Bailey if he wasn't distracted with his acting career. You were a normal guy in a normal world, you could call Valerie or Catherine and tell them you needed to crash. But who knows what this was. It could be nothing, but it could be bad.

Wingy Rosenzweig's place was a fortress, and he had offered.

"You want me to come get you?" Wingy asked.

"Meet me in the street, bring a coat. I'll be getting out of a big Caddy."

"How bad is it?"

"Maybe bad. Maybe some black cops want to get even. Maybe I'm hallucinating off the drugs and my heart surgery."

"I'll bring down my street sweeper and some Lorezpam. Fix you up either way," said Wingy. "Get you upstairs. Lock this place down."

"Give that Rottweiler of yours some Xanax or whatever," said Rook.

"No problem," said Wingy. "He don't live here anymore."

6

Rosenzweig was outside his brownstone when Sid Rosen double-parked his big Caddy. Instead of Wingy's guard dog with a bad attitude, there was a pair of bodyguards. Military types in long coats which meant they were carrying heavy.

"You want me to bring you in?" asked Sidney.

"Looks like we're okay here," Lucas told him.

"One's coming, one's going," said Rosenzweig. "But getting upstairs might be tough unless you got your legs back under you."

"I'll be alright."

"You call me if you need anything, Lucas boy. Meanwhile, rest up. You can catch up on your reading."

"Right," said Rook.

One of the long coats went back inside with Wingy. The other one helped Lucas up the stairs. Strong, with a hint of some accent from the couple of words he said when Lucas had to take a breather on the stairs. Then the first one came back down the steps and they mostly carried Lucas up to the apartment.

"Phil and Bill, the Glacas brothers," said Rosenzweig. "Can you believe it, looking like peas in a pod the way they do and their names rhyming? Anyway, neither one of them has crapped on the rug or bit the hand that feeds them."

"No, sir," said Phil. He took off his trench coat. Underneath was a hi-tech piece of machine gun.

"You expecting trouble, Wingy?" asked Lucas.

"Cost of doing some new business, Rook. Phil here's bonded and deductible. Right?"

"Anything you say, Mr. Rosenzweig." The bodyguard adjusted his rig and sat down in the chair he had placed to give him coverage of the front door and the windows.

"Tired? Hungry, Rook? A Reuben is indicated by your symptoms," said Wingy.

"I'm supposed to limit my cholesterol to less than 300 milligrams per day and my sodium to 2400."

"That's a heart attack diet, Rook. You have a heart attack?"

"Other than by three heavy rounds I didn't. But Dr. DiBona tells me 300 milligrams cholesterol tops and the sodium. I got to follow what he's telling me, at least until I'm on my feet."

"I'll get you a garden salad with tuna. That should be alright. Phil, you want anything?"

"The usual, Mr. R."

"He eats the same thing every meal. Roast beef on white, tomato and mayo and a diet ginger ale."

Lucas tried to make himself comfortable on the sofa, but the incisions hurt.

"You alright?"

"Just dandy. I may have to nod out for a couple of minutes here, alright?" said Lucas.

"Sure, sure. How long do you want to be out? You got meds to take or anything?"

"I'm good."

Rosenzweig passed him the comforter from the other end of the couch.

"I don't sleep so good," said Rook. "Ask Mr. Glacas here not to put me down if I'm restless."

"You hear that, Phil?"

"I do, Mr. R."

"And Rook, the Rotty, I didn't put him down," said Wingy. "He went back to the breeder."

"You sure it wasn't that farm every kid's pet winds up running free and chasing whatever?"

"I'm sure. You okay?" said Wingy.

"I'm good." Lucas Rook drifted off and then fell into his sleep, which had been not very good for a very long time. There were the usual freak shows that everybody on the job has. The redhead decapitated by a tractor trailer, the old man gone to worms in his bed. And here comes the freak with the tattooed eyes all over him, and that nice little old lady who was breaking little girls' necks and burned off Chick Misher's face. And there was seeing his twin brother, Kirk, bleed to death in front of the Sephora Club.

And now showing, Detective Dwight Graves, who looked like Bill Cosby and once was Hy Gromek's partner, telling him that his twin brother, Kirk, was on the take, then shooting him three times up close and leaving him for dead and the ambulance and the hospital. Except somehow all the evil shit was on him, Lucas Rook. And not for letting it happen, like not being able to keep Kirk alive or even from being a crooked cop like Graves had said his brother was. But somehow that *he* had done it, done it all himself. The shooting, the being shot, the dying, the lying, the crying for his own shit life.

"You alright?" asked Rosenzweig with his bodyguard standing next to him.

"Great," said Lucas as he woke up. "I dreamt I was at some fancy hotel and my croissant was stale."

"Better you sleep for more than fifteen minutes," said Wingy and they sat back down.

The buzzer rang. It was the delivery boy. "On the credit card, Mr. Rosenzweig? And the tip?"

"Sure," said Wingy. "Fifteen percent. Leave it on the landing if everything's there. Check the order, you were short the onion rings last time."

He said to Rook, "Phil will get the food. I'll get you some sweats to wear. You want to wash up?"

32

"I'm good. It'll be good to get some human clothes on again."

Rook and Wingy ate at the little table in the kitchen area. "You want something to calm you down, Lucas? Nobody knows drug interactions better than me, and there's nothing you could be taking that a little Xanax is going to interfere with. You got your meds with you?"

"I left them behind."

Rosenzweig took a bite of his pastrami on rye. "And you left why, if you want to tell me?"

"First there's cops outside my door, then there's not. Only black cops, which didn't seem like such a good idea since it was one of their own just got dead. Then there's nobody in the middle of the shift, which got me thinking." He picked up a fork full of the tuna, then put it down. "I had Sid bust me out."

Wingy took another bite of sandwich and a swig of cream soda. "Seems to me it's the trauma talking. They were going to discharge you when?"

"Soon."

"Probably a good idea for the hospital from an insurance perspective, which could bite you in the ass big time. You leave AMA, 'Against Medical Advice,' gives your insurer an excuse to deny all kinds of things. This stuff I know about. You should go back. At least to get your meds or chart, then get your doc to discharge you. I'll send Phil with you in case you're right about there being any odd shit going on."

"Which leaves you where, Wingy, if your pitbull comes with me?"

"Same as before. Part of the deal is they always have backup on call. Maybe I'll get lucky and they'll send a hot blonde named Jill."

"So you think I'm acting fucked up, Wingy? The drugs, whatever?"

"I do, my friend. Post-traumatic stress at the least. And with Phil coming with you, I think you're good."

Rook forced himself to eat something. "Probably that and all the drugs," he said. "Besides, you're the professional."

Phil's replacement, who happened to be named Max, was there in an hour. The four of them rode back to St. Vincent's, where Phil bypassed the alarm on the fire door and they helped Rook back upstairs into bed.

Doctor DiBona's resident came in just as Lucas was getting settled. "Glad you've decided to stay a little while longer. You'd have had us both in a jackpot."

"Just pushing my exercise a little bit too much, doc. Had to sit down in the lounge upstairs."

"You want anything before I head out?"

"I'm good," said Rook.

Phil said nothing.

DiBona was in at 6AM the next morning. Rook was up and ready to go. Glacas had not slept.

"Family member?" asked Dr. DiBona. "You have any questions, feel free."

"Okay," said Glacas.

Lucas convinced the doc that he was good to go, and DiBona went over the discharge instructions, including the reminder to wear the Ted Hose. He also went over the meds, including the possible side effects such as unusual bleeding or bruising.

"Mine or theirs?" Rook asked.

"I hope neither. None of these medications are long term as you did not have a heart attack per se. I'm also going to write you for Lorazepam, for anxiety or sleep."

"You think I need that?"

"Most patients do. Especially those who aren't used to taking it easy, the kind who might skip out of the hospital in the middle of the night. And PTSD, Post-Traumatic Stress Disorder, is real. Anxiety, depression, paranoia, anywhere up to six months. Longer than that, it's something else. You need anything, call me, 24/7, even if you've got an inkling it's an emergency, which I don't expect. Otherwise, I'll see you at our follow-up."

Phil helped Lucas Rook get his belongings together after the discharge paperwork was done and drove him to his apartment at the Hotel St. Claire without any discussion other than directions.

The new deskman's name was Ouma. Ribai had either moved on up or found himself in a frying pan for having no green card.

"I'm so glad you're okay," said the Martha Raye look-alike tenant on the elevator. "What a nasty, nasty set of circumstances." As they came to her floor, she leaned forward. "Fourth floor," she said. "Pots and pans." Then she got off.

The bodyguard insisted on unlocking Rook's door and going through the place. At least the crime tape was off Gracey's door across the hall.

The NYPD had confiscated all of Rook's guns except the throwdown .38 he had under the floorboards in his bedroom. Just fine with the Black Talon rounds, which had been illegal for years because of their kill power. "Black Felon" they called them. First thing, get the job to get its head out of its ass and return his iron or it's off to the toy store for new shit.

"Mr. Rosenzweig said I'm supposed to finish out my shift here," said Glacas.

"I'm too tired to argue," said Rook. "Meanwhile, the cable works and there's a beer in the fridge."

"Not while I'm working."

"Of course not. I'll have yours on my Rice Krispies in the morning."

Lucas Rook went to sleep and got through the night even with all the bad shit. Grace Savoy's phone call woke him up.

"What are you doing, Gracey?" asked Rook.

"Still under 'the man's' control, but it's okay except they think I'm cuckoo, cuckoo."

"You got a good lawyer, Gracey?"

"I guess so. I got a good lawyer, Russell Spritzer."

"I want you to talk to Warren Phelps, the best," Rook told her.

"Okey dokey," she said. "Especially since they're charging me with murder."

7

Detective Antopol was parked downstairs while his partner was at the chiropractor getting his lower back adjusted. Stanley fired up a cigarette and turned to face out the window, as much to eyeball the citizenry as to avoid a later conversation about him stinking up the unmarked. About a thousand people walked by on cell phones, all talking crap about what so and so said or who was fucking who or some big business deal. Maybe somebody was talking to his soon-to-be ex and exchanging cunt lessons.

Two smokes and some *New York Post*, his partner was down.

"You alright?" he asked Carillo.

"Good, except the check I had to write. As fast we get the union to cover shit, the chiro's are coming up with another way to describe it so it's not scheduled."

Antopol pulled into traffic. "Never believed in that stuff anyways, except what's-his-name, that Jewish guy, Cohen, moved to Jersey, said he got a spinal adjustment he could fuck like a stallion afterward."

"The one whose partner took out Bambi Cabresa?"

"The very same."

Detective Carillo reached into his inside pocket for a small envelope and took out a piece of candy.

"Sharing is caring," said Antopol.

"Candy corn." Joey bit off the little white end of one. "It's crazy or like that, but it calms me down, like you do with them smokes except they don't stink up our unit. They remind me of little teeth, and I eat them first the white, then the orange, then the yellow. Like they're little chickens' teeth. Like you got your smoking, only these candy corns won't be the cause of their taking my lung out."

Antopol hit his siren to get some Long Island shoppers to give up their double park.

"Fridman had half his lung out and he never smoked, not one time," said Stanley.

"Fair enough," said Carillo. "Now let's generate enough work from the Graves job that we can take lost time for a year and nobody gives a shit."

Jack Welby from Uptown was sitting in the lobby when Antopol and Carillo came in. "Well, now us New York's finest got the place surrounded," he said.

"You win a lottery for this cushy off-the-clock or you score it because of your good looks?" asked Antopol.

Welby reached for his smokes. "You guys get this for five minutes, let me catch a blow."

"I'll walk you out," said Stanley.

"Nice of me, ain't it," said Joey. He went over to the front desk and got a copy of the tenant list with one of his hard looks. "I'm keeping this or you're making me a copy, and you're not calling anybody up about nothing. You savvy?"

"I understand the meaning of your gold badge," said Ouma.

Antopol came back and they started the interviews. They got mostly useless background and some bad attitude from the hundred-and-eighty-pound lovely in the velvet bow who did not want to be late for her jazzercise class.

"I absolutely do not have time for this," said Ms. Velvet Hair Bow. "And don't you need a warrant or something?"

"Only if we're searching your place," said Antopol. "And then we'd be leaving it in absolute shambles."

"Shambles," said Joey. "But all we're doing is asking you about Miss Savoy and what happened."

"About that I can talk. A prostitute, a whore at the very least. I don't even think she's really blind, to tell you the truth."

"She have many visitors?" asked Carillo.

"My husband and I, Leonard Teitlebaum, are new to the city. Connecticut is fine if you're raising kids, but Manhattan…"

"What about the other people who live on her floor?"

"The man in the leather coat, I heard he was shot too, Mafia. My husband's sure of that."

Her phone rang. "I have to take this," she said.

"She has to take this," said Stanley.

"By the way, partner," said Detective Carillo. " 'Shambles' is an excellent word. I plan to use it regularly. 'Hands up, dirtbag, or I'll make a shambles out of you.' "

Mrs. Teitlebaum finished her call. She was quite agitated. "My yoga class is cancelled. I fully expect to be reimbursed by the City."

"How do you figure that?" asked Carillo.

"Fully," she repeated.

"Absolutely," said Antopol. "We'll see you get the paperwork within the next forty-eight hours."

She took some deep bullshit breaths. Her eyebrows fluttered. She did some more of the breathing, then spoke with her eyes still closed. "There's another tenant on that floor, a retired man who does something with butterflies, but I understand he's been in Florida for some time."

Antopol and Carillo moved on. There was Mr. Funchion, who was day trading on his computer. Mrs. Moscowitz, who smelled like stale cigarettes and thought she was a comedian. Her place smelled like mothballs. Cats meowed in 4F, but they didn't answer the door. A hospice nurse was the only hit on the 5th floor. And they got some irrelevant tidbits from the retired math teacher before it was time to accidentally pay Ms. Savoy's apartment a visit, where they shouldn't be because they know she lawyered up and the search warrant hadn't been signed yet since apparently every judge in the world was at some Bar Convention thing.

A blind man opened the door. "Can I help you?" he said.

"We're police detectives," said Carillo.

"You're aware she's represented by counsel, gentlemen, I'm sure. And that would be me. And unless you have the appropriate paperwork, I must assume you are here in error…"

"No problem, Counselor. We got the wrong place."

"Of course you did. Now if you'll excuse me." Spritzer closed the door.

"Arrogant prick, Joey. That's for sure. Not to mention why's he in her apartment."

"They're like that," said Carillo. "Fellow gets dealt a bad hand, he walks around like he's some kind of hero."

"Meatball hero at that," said Stanley. "While we're at it, let's see if the butterfly man is really not here and maybe Lucas Rook is."

The elevator stopped. A girl with a big plastic cart got out. Joey tinned her primarily because of her big not-plastic tits showing through her blouse.

"Did I do something wrong?" she said.

"Do you think you did?"

"Nothing that I care to talk about."

"Meaning what?" asked Detective Carillo.

"Smoke some weed. Get it on with anything in pants."

Antopol lifted the drop cloth on her cart. "What is all this shit? We talking hydroponics in there?"

"Not hardly." She handed over her card. "Flutterbyes Are Us."

"Flutterbyes?"

"For butterflies, obviously. What I have here is small sponges and paper towels, toothpicks, Oasis foam, milkweed for the Monarchs, dill for the Black Swallowtails, feeding solution of one part sugar, two parts water, Gatorade, and as you can see, one can of Black Label."

"You growing weed in there, right?"

"Nope, butterflies. Dr. Haimowitz is not in, but his hobby is. And the beer's for me before it gets skunky. You don't mind caterpillars and flying things, come on in." She put the key in the lock. "Especially if you like watching my ass while I work."

"I better go with her," said Antopol.

They gave the place a once-over just to keep it kosher.

"Creepy in there," Stanley said when he came out. "Like that Alfred Hitchcock movie."

"They were birds, partner, in that movie."

"Same difference."

"All that talk got you thirsty?" asked Carillo.

"That it does, Joseph. Especially since I got girlie's phone number. Let's canvass that saloon around the corner."

"We check Rook's not still in the hospital while we're here?" Carillo asked.

"I'm creeped out enough with all them bugs and what not. No need I'm looking at his tubes and on an empty stomach if he is here," said Antopol.

"Done," said his partner. "We shall return."

Detective Welby was busy earning his off the clock when they got down to the lobby. "You two lawmen see the pair of knockers just came in? I'd motorboat those bad boys until New Year's."

"Really?" said Stanley.

"Didn't notice," said Carillo.

"You boys coming back, bring me a burger or something. I get no relief on this detail."

"What they paying you, Jack, 30 an hour?"

"That's about right," Welby said.

"We ain't eaten yet. You buy, we bring," said Antopol.

"You're killing me," said Welby as he handed over a twenty.

41

"We'll see what we can do," Carillo told him.

The two detectives went around the corner to the Eagle II and had a pitcher with a couple of roast beef sandwiches and got Welby's to go. Then they went to Rook's apartment. Glacas opened the door.

"Two of New York's finest," said Lucas when he saw who it was. "You collecting for the Benevolent Association, I'm all out of change."

"You're not going to invite us to your pity party," said Antopol.

Glacas blocked their entry.

"Tell your doorman to move," said Carillo.

"It's okay," Lucas said. "They're here to squeeze my shoes."

"Just got to write this up, Rook," said Stanley. "We'll be out of here."

"You give us what you got's fine, you know that," said Joey.

"I got post traumatic whatever, other than Dwight and me used to be on the same job and he puts three into me, after which he's going to do my blind neighbor who's got my gun, I don't know how the fuck that happens. And she beats him to it, which is how she and me both ain't deader than shit and DG is."

"You got anything else?" asked Carillo.

"Shot is plenty," said Lucas.

"We're done here," said Antopol. "Let's go write this up."

"You should've brought me a tray of cookies or something, fellas," Lucas said, but they had gone.

Glacas waited at the door for the two detectives to return. They didn't.

"You can roll," Lucas told him. "Those two will be keeping an eye on my place for a while."

"That's between you and Mr. Rosenzweig. Otherwise I'm here 'til tomorrow morning."

Rook got Wingy on the phone as he was beginning an audition for the replacement of the blowjob girl who had given him the runny dick.

"You do me the favor, Lucas, of letting my man work his shift. Tomorrow or the next day you should be good enough you don't need him. Unless you got a temp or seeing double or whatever. You got any trouble with your wounds, I just got Vancomycin in. You call me."

Rook hung up and went back into the bedroom. "I'm going to get what passes for sleep, Phil, Bill, whatever. You hear me making noise or whatever, let me know it's you before you come in." Rook popped a cold one, took his pain meds, and lay down.

You're a cop, you never sleep right. They have your body rhythms all crossed up and you're grabbing a half hour, forty-five minutes on the clock so you don't nod-out or have the reflexes of an old man and get somebody else or yourself killed like a dog in the street. Then somewhere along the way you're going to see something that's going to be in your head like a tumor forever, an old lady with her head rotted out or six-year-old boy with blood running down the back of his legs.

And if you're Lucas Rook you've got a double, triple feature going on, one being your twin brother bleeding out in front of you, which has enough crazy shit to make *Freaks*, which you saw one day while trying to ball an NYU chick, it makes them look like *The Sound of Music* or whatever. So now you're shot by the same fuckface who tells you your brother's on the take. Also you absolutely got that post traumatic stress shit so when you do fall asleep you're dreaming that you're being chased and doing the chasing at the same time, except you feel like you got the shit scared out of you either way.

All this has you up figuring out how you're going to break into Tanners to get new iron or into the property room at the precinct house to get your guns back.

"Coming out," Lucas said so the bodyguard he didn't ask for and didn't want, didn't add to the gunshots he was dealing with.

Glacas was watching television with the sound off. Dedicated. And smart too.

The bad leg, compliments of Etillio, who was appropriately dead, and his chest, thanks to Dwight Graves' three rounds, were a joyful adjunct to the gift of pissing in the middle of the night. "Adjunct," a Catherine Wren word. She invited him as an "Adjunct Visiting Professor" to her university once, which meant he gave a little reality talk to a course called "Writing the Noir," whatever that was. College kids except for Jeanie Oren were for shit. So was peeing on your sweat pants.

"Good job. I'm halfway to the home," he said out loud.

"You say something?" asked Glacas.

"I'm good," said Rook. "Couldn't be better."

The bodyguard was still watching the television with the sound off when Rook made his grand entrance, fresh from washing off the pee smell with the wet end of his towel.

"You do good work, Glacas," he said.

"That's what Mr. Rosenzweig pays me for."

"I'm going around the corner for some eggs. Or going to try anyways. You want breakfast?"

"I have breakfast with my brother," Phil said. He looked at his watch. "I got another half hour. I'll sit with you."

Rook put on his windbreaker and his .38 in the pocket. The .357 that Gracey had used to take out DG, it made sense they took those, but his Glocks, his carry piece and his back-up, they were just busting his balls in confiscating that.

"You give me a lift, I can make a stop."

"I could do that," said Glacas.

The elevator stopped twice on the way down. Phil let an old lady in, but kept between her and Rook and told a man in an overcoat that he'd have to take the next elevator up.

The lobby of the St. Claire was busy, but there wasn't an off-duty sitting there. Likely as not, one of the bosses or IAB had decided to bust Welby's balls and kill it for him and whoever else for not going through the Department's Paid Retail Unit to get approved side work.

"Houston Street," Lucas said when they were inside Glacas' SUV.

When they got to Tanner's, the gun shop was closed. There was a note on a shirt cardboard with a 305 phone number to call and to contact Herbie's in Monroe if you have any inventory to pick up. Monroe, New York, home of the radical Hasids and the Jehovah Witnesses. Only in America.

Tanner's closed meant his kidneys probably shut down altogether. Good guy and with a great old lady who could shoot the eye out of Jack of hearts. Tomorrow he'd get Sid to run him over to Fort Lee to Leavitt's. A little more paperwork to be buying in Jersey, but Leavitt was stand-up like the Tanners. Also Fort Lee was the home of the warm and generous Ms. Valerie Moon, which meant maybe a gun in his hand, his gun in hers. In the meantime, breakfast at Joe Oren's and his .38 would do.

"You change your mind?" Lucas asked him. "They make breakfast like it's dinner."

"My duty isn't over. I'll have coffee."

Working until the last minute of his shift was done. Only way to do it. McCullagh, his training officer, had told him the first day, "You leave your post ten seconds early or before the next cop comes on, something's going to go down and ruin your career, not to mention somebody's life."

Jeanie Oren was behind the counter and she came running out to meet him.

"Sit at a booth," she said. "Let me get you a cup of coffee. I mean two." Jeanie started to walk away and then turned around. She was crying.

Sam came out of the back.

"Well, how you feeling?" he said. "You look like you're doing good. Good enough to have an omelet of mine, put some steak *and* ham in that, get your blood up strong again."

"Good, Sam, that's good."

Phil Glacas turned to the window. An SUV with blacked-out windows pulled up. Rook's hand went to his revolver.

"That'll be my brother," Phil said.

Bill Glacas came in the coffee shop. Built the same, with the same military walk and from the looks of it, the same vest and automatic weapon under his coat.

"Chow's on me," Lucas told the one at his table.

"We're good," said Phil. "You need me or my brother to stay, I'll call Mr. Rosenzweig."

"I'm good," Lucas told him.

"Take care now," said the first Glacas. He looked at his watch. "Let's roll, little brother."

After the second cup of Sam's good coffee, Rook felt almost half alive. He ate the omelet with Jeanie sitting in the booth with him.

"Do you feel alright?" she asked.

Lucas Rook thought about a lot of things, about how old she was and why the thought had entered his head about grabbing her arm when she one time leaned in to touch his face.

"Your dad around?" he asked her.

"Daddy was going to see a supplier. I heard him arguing with them over the phone."

He handed Jeanie a ten dollar bill and went into the kitchen.

"Appreciate the breakfast, Samuel," he said.

"You let me do the cooking, I'll have you pissing smoke in a week," the cook said. He handed over a take-out container of soup. "And you eat hot sauce three times a day. Take that no matter what the doctors are telling you."

Rook left through the back. Maybe go up to his office at 166 Fifth or at least see Jimbo Turner for a shine. Let the world know he was back at it and get some business going, even if he was walking slow. After, stop at Sid Rosen's. Have a drink, shoot the shit, ride out to the police home to see Tuze. The bottom fell out. He felt weak and tired. Time to go back and get some beddy-bye. He waited for the cab with his hand on his .38.

8

The sign on Sid's garage the next morning said "back in an hour," which told Rook he was either really going for parts or going to get his part lubricated. Soo's pretend Jewish deli was a block away and his cabbage soup, somewhere halfway between *kimchee* and what Mayor Koch's mother used to make, would hit the spot. So would Soo's daughter Sonny, who was somewhere between hot Asian chick and hot New York chick.

"The usual," Lucas told her.

Sonny came out from behind the counter, skin tight jeans, bare midriff. "It's hot," she said.

"I can see that," said Lucas.

"The soup too. You should call me."

"As soon as I figure out how to be twenty-eight again."

"I'll help you with that," she said.

A fat guy from ConEd got up to leave, so Lucas Rook sat down, ate the soup and a sandwich, and called in to pick up his messages, of which there were none.

Back at his apartment, a note under the door from building management that he would read in a week or so. He took off his Kevlar, which was not crazy to wear if you just took three rounds and had your heart operated on. Then he got into bed, too beat down for the sofa.

He woke up wet. Bleeding out, he peed himself, sweating from infection. All lovely choices. It was the bottle of water he had left on the nightstand. Lucas got up and made it into the bathroom to take a leak standing up, one of Man's greatest accomplishments, and then lay down again on the couch with his .38 and the killer ammo, two of his best friends.

He fell back asleep quicker and deeper than he had hoped for and didn't awake until the phone rang. It was Gransback from building management.

"We knocked, Mr. Rook, but no one answered. Did you get our note?"

"I think last time I checked I was recuperating over being shot. And who's 'we'?" Lucas said.

"We is me, Mr. Rook. On behalf of the new management, we, they, have been trying to contact you. May I please come by?"

Rook stayed on the sofa, but shifted into a sitting position. "I don't think you want to see me with all the tubes running in and out of me, which is how I spend the day. So if you're here to tell me you're going to be giving me notice about having to buy or leave, now's not the time. It wouldn't look very good. Or feel that good either, Mr. Gransback."

"On the contrary, we're hoping that you'll be staying on."

"How's that?"

"That's what I wish to speak to you about. But perhaps later in the day or tomorrow. I'm sorry to have disturbed you."

My heavens, what a change of approach. First they're squeezing him about how he's going to come up with the financing, which he talks to the credit union about. Even Gracey and Wingy Rosenzweig. Then he gets popped up on their roof and bingo, they're good Samaritans. Time to talk to a lawyer for this. You got either slick trickster Felix Gavilan, who's looking to sue anything that breathes, and you got Warren G. Phelps, who has you kissing his ring that he's pulled out of his fancy top hat the same rabbit he put in there. Either way, the real estate pricks who are taking the building condo got something in mind, and he's got to be ready to deal with them.

Lucas put on some coffee and took a shower the way the docs had told him, careful not to have the water too hot or stay too long. His answering machine was blinking when he got out. Catherine Wren saying that if he felt better they could go on a little picnic. Right, how about out on the patio where he got shot up and Dwight got dead. Maybe Central Park if they could time it right to get in the middle of some jigaboo wilding.

He called Sid Rosen for a ride out to the police home to see Tuze and then to the gun shop, but he got Sid's machine. "I am out getting parts, but if you're planning to pay your bill, I'll be returning." Always a charmer. Lucas picked up a message from the office, Owls Miksis saying that he had something new. In any case, you're in the City you got to have more than an illegal throwdown to keep you company. He tried the garage again.

"I was out getting my parts," Rosen said.

"I hear you, Sid. Can you run me over to Fort Lee and to see Tuze?"

"Sure I can, Lucas boy. We can get the Avanti out, see how she's running."

Terrific. Somebody else driving 'cause I'm shot, and he's driving my dead brother's car.

"You got an appetite we can stop along the way. Get some chili. I'll swing by and get you. You mind Bear comes along I put a blanket on the back seat?"

"That's fine, Sidney. We can make it a regular holiday, like a picnic."

The black fiberglass coupe ran a little hot and the brakes squealed, but the garageman told Rook it was nothing. "I got that Bendix kit straightened out. Their fault, not mine. They made it good. I'll check the thermostat when we get back."

Leavitt's Sportsman Shop was as open and inviting as Tanner's was a fortress, but then again this was Jersey, not Manhattan. Lots of fishing tackle, coolers and shotguns. Mannequins dressed up in cammy and fluorescent vests next to aluminum boats. The two grandsons were working the floor. The wife of one of the sons was working the register.

The old man was sitting in an aluminum lawn chair in the back. "Long time no see. You coming out here to buy some fishing crap or something else?"

"Else," said Rook. "Rock around the Glock, Benjamin."

"Even for you I'm not getting up. You see how nice and smooth my skin is, it's from the hormones they're giving me so my prostate cancer don't come back. I got a comfortable seat, so you go take a look. First door on the right. You looking for my son, he's out on the track pretending he's not robbing me blind." He underhanded Lucas the keys. "See how they handle. No range anymore, the insurance made me close that down."

There was some good stuff and some freaky shit. A G24 with a mag extension and Halo sight painted red, white, and blue was a little too much. So was the Smith and Wesson 50 cal with a three-inch barrel. Good enough to stop a truck, but maybe you got to be one to handle it, which right now he wasn't exactly there yet.

Money was tight, but Lucas needed at least a carry and a backup. The .38 would go back under the floorboards. He picked out a Model 21. Thirteen rounds of .45 would be more than enough and a 36C on sale.

"Your weapon there got the ports, you know. Buying it for a beginner or a lady?" said Leavitt. "Lots of them coming around."

"Buying it 'cause it's on sale, Ben."

"I could do better for you on something's not Glock, which I don't particularly like to stock anyway. They say 'Austrian,' but we both know what that is."

Sid Rosen walked over. He had a fishing hat and was carrying two bags of beef jerky. "Figure I hang out the 'Gone Fishing' sign, I should look the part. Jerky's for Bear."

"For bear?" asked Leavitt. "I can fix you right up. Fifty cal. Stop Smokey in his tracks."

"I'm good," said Sid.

Lucas took out the cash. Ben Leavitt looked over at Rosen.

"Going to see you got any something or others," said Sidney.

Lucas signed enough sleight-of-hand paperwork for him to walk out of the gun store and have his weapons legal.

"Nice doing business with you, Benjamin," he said.

"Everything's nice. You're paying cash and today I don't have to worry about my schvontz falling off." He adjusted himself on the lawn chair. "You see my kid, tell him no hurry coming back."

Rook dry swallowed two Percs when they started up again and tried to doze, but leaning his head against the window pulled on his incision. "Think we should pass on the Tex-Mex, Sid," he said.

"Should've taken the Merc. Maybe my Towne Car," said Sid. "You good to go out to see your friend?"

"I'm good here if your dog's okay."

"Bear's fine. The mufflers remind him of his mother."

"They do?" asked Rook.

"They do. Like putting an alarm clock near a pup."

Lucas drifted in and out until they got to where Ray Tuzio was crapping and sleeping away the rest of his life. Sid got out to walk Bear as Lucas went in.

"No dogs allowed," yelled the security guard at the front door.

"K-9," said Lucas, which shut the guy up.

They had moved Tuze since Rook was there last. A couple of weeks and the moron at the front desk is telling you the man who taught you the streets, saved your life, is now in the "Old Timers" wing.

Lucas went back to the Alzheimer's Department. An actual nurse back there, and doors that had to be buzzed open.

"Mr. Tuzio is resting now," Nurse Shaw said after Rook went through the gymnastics of having to prove that he was entitled to know jack shit.

"I'm going to look in on Tuze," he said. "I'll be by Tuesdays and Fridays," Lucas told her. "To make sure he's alright and that he got those sunglasses of his. Or maybe Mondays and Wednesdays."

"I understand," Nurse Shaw said. "I do."

"That's more than Tuze does."

Sid could see that Rook was in the drinking mood and not the talking mood when he came out. He found a place called Joe's Famous and they threw back enough shots to dull anybody's mind. Then no conversation or radio until they got back into Manhattan, when Sidney turned on Michael Savage, who was talking about all the good turning the other cheek did for Jesus.

"That's what I'm talking about," said the garageman.

Rook's cell rang. It was Owls Miksis again.

"Can't keep the job open longer," he said. "You got to let me know or I go to the next swinging dick on the list."

"What we got?" Lucas said.

"Nothing heavy. The kind of job you hate. The usual jealous spouse. This time there's a little more spice. The cheater's a lady vice principal at some fancy private school doing the horizontal mambo with a faculty member. The hubby wants to pay her back what she deserves. What he gives us is the boy-toy still lives with his parents, so they're doing the nasty at a motel in Jersey. He wants stills, video. A kicker if we get audio, her screaming she wants more or talking with her mouth full. Fifty an hour's the best I can do unless we get some good sound."

Lucas went over the numbers in his head. With Owls he only did business in person and in cash, which meant probably two trips out to West 159th Street where Miksis still had his office. He made you sit there an hour while he told the same stories about the Polo Grounds. Bobby Thompsons' shot heard round the world, Matty, the groundskeeper, who lived with his family in an apartment under the left field stands.

The lovebirds were screwing their brains out in Jersey, which meant he was going to need somebody to do the driving for the next week until he got the clearance from Doc DiBona or whatever. Plus there was the surveillance equipment. Maybe he could lay the outside work off to somebody else like Welby or Dunlop. But you need wiggle room to do that and keep a slice, and Owl's numbers had no wiggle room.

"I need seventy," Rook told him. "Reimbursement for equipment rental."

"I need to pay you sixty. Okay on the rental thing."

"Deal," said Lucas. "Can I swing by now?"

"That's why they call me Owls," Miksis said.

Sid made the detour and took the dog around the block a couple of times while Lucas got the file and the initial payment. When Rook got back to his apartment, he took some index cards and opened a file. Then he took another two Percocets and lay down.

9

Lucas slept until noon. He was getting out of the shower when the phone rang. It was Catherine Wren.

"I'm downstairs, Lucas," she said. "I brought you soup."

"I'm not…"

"I know I should have called," she said. "But you would've only told me no."

"Cat…" he started.

"I'm coming up," she said. "I don't want this to get cold."

Rook pulled the sheet off his sofa. No time to shave, but she always liked the rough look, which hopefully did something to cancel the half dead look. He thought about taking his .45 off the mantelpiece, she always hated that, but after all it was such an essential to the décor.

A knock on the door, a woman's hand. He waited until she spoke.

"Florence Nightengale," she said.

Lucas let Catherine in. Her hands were trembling.

"You don't like the beatnik look?" Lucas said. "All artsy-fartsy?"

She went into the kitchenette area.

"Can you find everything?" he called. No answer. He went in to the little kitchen. She was crying.

He put his arm around her. She pulled away.

"I'm okay," he said. "I'm just a little out of shape is all." He took the soup. "I got a microwave."

"One of them has meat in it. I thought you'd like that." She started to cry again, then deep sobs.

"Crying's good for you," Rook said. "It opens up your sinuses." He handed her a napkin from the paper bag.

Catherine kissed him and then put the soup in to heat up. " 'It lets the sad out of you,' Lucas Rook. Rosey Grier said that. You know, the football player. I'm sad you're hurt. And that you won't let me take care of you."

He pressed the buttons on the microwave. "It helps if you turn it on, Catherine. Rosey Grier was Bobby's bodyguard. I'll tell you about that job someday, RFK in the kitchen."

Catherine Wren started to cry again. "It's just not right, Lucas. It's not right," she said. She took a deep breath. "Now let's sit down."

Lucas cleared off a space on the little dining bar.

"I'll make some tea," she said.

"I've got thirty, forty kinds," he told her. "Herbal, floral, medicinal. You name it, as long as it's Lipton. I even have soup bowls around here somewhere."

"I should have brought something else," she said. "Maybe some bagels and a smear."

"A *schmir*. A *smear,* that's some kind of woman's test. In New York, cream cheese, some kind of spread, is called a *schmir.*"

"I'm sorry, Lucas."

"It's alright, Cat. It's probably not for me anyway, the cholesterol."

"No, no, I'm sorry you're in pain. I'm sorry you got hurt." She turned away and then back again. "I'm sorry we're not together."

"We are together. We're having soup and tea. And talking about…"

She started toward the bedroom. "I'm packing. You're coming to stay with me."

Rook followed her. "I've got work to do, Catherine."

She was picking things up, making the bed. There was a beer can on the night table. "Are you supposed to be drinking, Lucas? I don't think so."

He sat down. "Beer's not drinking, and it was from before. Besides, beer's got B vitamins or something, and it's good. It helps you piss."

She sat down on the bed. "Please come home with me. We could have walks together. That would be good for you. And you could rest." She opened one of his bureau drawers.

"I've got to work, Cat. I got bills to pay."

"I'll lend you the money, or something, until you're, you know. I don't want you to get hurt again."

Lucas started to laugh, then stopped. "First, I'm not taking any money from you. Second, the job's not anything anybody's going to get hurt."

"You're probably going to be fighting some mobsters or something."

"Not hardly. Some loser cheating on her husband."

"And you probably shouldn't be doing that either. What happens if…"

"Here's what's going to happen, Catherine. I'm going to drive out to the motel. I'm going to lay some Jeffersons on the desk clerk. Tape them doing the nasty, write it up and then pay my rent with their sordid interlude. You like that word, 'interlude'?"

"You're going to do this work thing, aren't you?"

"I am, Cat. It will be fine."

"Can I smoke out on your veranda?" she asked.

"My patio? Sure you can. Just watch out if there's a naked blind girl. She's a killer."

"Okay, then," Catherine said.

When she came back in Lucas was confirming the arrangements for the per diem surveillance equipment from Zorro's on Third Avenue. People think you're a PI you've got all the surveillance stuff, but that's only if you work industrial espionage which nowadays only the big boys get. You got your contacts, the computer, and your street skills are usually enough for what he's doing.

"Can I persuade you to come home with me?" Catherine asked when she came back in.

"Let me make you an offer, Cat. You come out with me. A lovely ride to picturesque Englewood, New Jersey's finest motel."

"Do we put a glass against the wall and listen? That might be a turn-on."

"Not unless the sound of rutting pigs does it for you. Anyway, all we're going to do is scope the place out." He went in to dress. "We can stop at Slavitt's and get a good steak. I get my strength up, I'll show you what smutty can be. Only thing is I can't do the driving. You mind?"

"That's the first time you ever asked me for help, Lucas Rook."

"Well, maybe I'm catching on here, Catherine."

She brought her Beamer around and they went out and picked up the surveillance shit. Then out the Westside Highway to 195 and to Route 4.

They were early for dinner at Slavitt's so they went on to the motel. Lucas had her park in the back. "Scumbags run a game getting plate numbers off of lovebirds then squeezing them."

"We lovebirds, Lucas Rook?"

"Sure we are, Cat. That's for sure." He folded up a twenty for the palm of his hand. "Another lesson, you shake hands like this, you make a lot of friends."

Rook went around to the check-in and fast-tinned the clerk. "I'm guessing you short-sheeting the rooms and not doing your legal duty about getting the proper names and addresses of your patrons. Very serious, post 9-11."

The desk clerk looked like Gilligan from the TV show. "Am I in trouble?" he asked.

"That depends."

"Depends on what?"

Lucas showed him the photo of the boy-toy. "You know him?"

"I've seen him."

"And you didn't get his proper ID, now did you."

Gilligan looked away.

"Well, it's your lucky day. All you got to do is cooperate and you'll be alright. This is a civil matter with possible criminal implications."

The desk clerk lit a cigarette and took a deep drag.

"Not allowed to smoke here either," Rook said. "You're making this hard on yourself."

"What do I have to do?"

"I'll go check with my superior and be back in a couple of hours," Lucas told him.

Lucas kept the twenty. Gilligan was a pussy. He took Catherine Wren to dinner and a couple glasses of wine. Then they went back to Gilligan's Island.

The lamp with the camera and recorder he had gotten from Zorro's would do just fine. Rook announced that if the lovebirds showed up, the deskman was to plug it in on the night table, then take it out after they left. Lucas would check with him every other day and as a cooperating citizen he would be compensated for his services. Everything works out and he does what he's supposed to do, he gets a hundred. They come in, the lamp goes on. He calls. The lamp comes out. He's noted up.

"I'll do that," said the deskman. "You had me scared there for a while."

"I can do that," said Rook as he handed him the twenty. "I surely can."

"Everything okay?" Catherine asked when he got into the car.

"Swell, Cat. Business as usual," he told her.

They went back to Rook's, where he let Catherine do most of the work. Then they turned on the television and watched the news. The second story was a press conference, Captain Leonard announcing that Grace Savoy had been transferred from the hospital to the jail at Rikers Island.

10

You're a cop as long as he was, you can tell when it's going wrong. He had Catherine Wren drop him off at Gracey's lawyer.

"Please, please reconsider about coming to stay with me," Catherine said.

"Let me sort out this, Cat. Then it would be good."

She leaned over to kiss him goodbye. Lucas kissed her back, but his face had already changed.

"I'll call you," he said.

Spritzer's office was a walk-up. Thick railings, good treads on the steps, what you'd expect for a blind man. Inside was what you'd expect, but only if you were at the circus.

The receptionist had only one arm, and when the secretary took Rook to the conference room, she wobbled. The lawyer made Rook wait, but apologized when he came in.

"I'm sorry," he said. "I was not expecting you and I have a closing in twenty minutes."

"Maybe *you* should be closing, Counselor. I can get you're not *seeing* this coming, Gracey at Rikers. Meanwhile you got your blind head up your ass."

"I'm inured to sight jokes, Mr. Rook, and I do appreciate you're Grace's friend, but I will not be bullied."

"That's a nice thing to call it," Lucas said. "I was going to say blindsided ass-fucked, but that's what Gracey got."

Spritzer sat down. "I have been in regular contact with the district attorney's office."

"That chinky smartass who's handling her case now? I checked."

"Mr. Eng and his superiors. Other than that I really can't discuss her case with you in greater detail."

"You can stuff your attorney-client privilege up your ass and tell me what you were doing that let her get moved to Rikers?"

"I did what my client instructed me to do."

"Right, which you're telling me is squat. There's a dozen things you could have done about it, including call me. Anything happens to her, you'll have more than your license to worry about."

"Or what, Mr. Rook? And I'm writing this down."

"Write this down, Mr. Blindass Lawyerman. You get in my way, I'll beat you so bad you won't be able to hear either."

"I don't respond to threats, Mr. Rook, I told you that. You should leave."

"No problem, Counselor," said Lucas Rook. "And I don't make threats, I give warnings. And if you're half as smart as you think you are, you'll stay the fuck out of my way."

Rook knew two men well enough at Rikers that he could call them to look after Gracey. There was a boss in Department of Corrections who owed him, but you do that, it's just as likely to cause someone down the line to get a hair up their ass. He called Bobby Perez, who had moved up the ladder when Tony Serra got pinched for tax evasion, they say, for using DOC employees to fix up his house and to work on Pataki's campaign. A hundred-fourteen count indictment? What was that really about? Lucas got Perez.

"How's life on the Rock, Robert?"

"It's beautiful, Rook. I got lawsuits all over the place that we closed up the gay dorms and I'm getting bombarded about opening a McDonald's here. Can you imagine what that's going to do?"

"Meanwhile you got 15,000 happy campers cutting each other up and trying to find true love and justice against all odds."

"You got it. What can I do for you?"

"Grace Savoy."

"Couple of cops got shot, including you. She's here."

"She's a friend of mine, Bobby."

"I hear you. You coming in?"

"I'm on my way."

"I'll put out the milk and cookies," Perez said and he hung up.

Rook also called Reggie Emery, who was on the boom squad. You're working ESU, outside or inside, you had to be a tough guy. Reggie had done both. 6'3", 250, black as the ace of spades and working towards his second pension and his master's degree. The conversation was brief, Rook letting him know that Gracey was good people and that he was on his way in. Reggie saying that he was hoping to get transferred to Oakpoint they ever get around to opening it.

"Sorry I got to run, Rook," Emery said. "It's time I put some fine citizen back into the bing. You're spending 23 hours a day in your 12x15 heaven, you're not too happy about getting stuffed back in. You get here, tell any of the blue and whites you're here to see Big Poppa. They'll know where I am."

"Big Poppa? Nice ring to it, Reg. I'll talk on you."

There was the dollar bus or mooching another ride. Rook took a cab back to Rosen's garage.

"I need the Merc, Sid."

"Can I run you someplace?" the garageman said.

"Going out to Rikers."

"Back working, Lucas boy?"

"They got Gracey out there. I'm rolling."

"I can run you out in a half hour. Got doctor what's-his-name coming by to pick up his piece of shit Saab."

Rosen went and got the big sedan out of the back bay.

Rikers Island, four hundred acres of skels awaiting trial or serving under a year, old heads and young punks. All of them pieces of shit, passing their AIDS around, cutting each other up with broken bathroom tiles and other handmade shanks. You don't have the East River and 12 foot high levees there for nothing. Some bleeding heart liberal said Rikers was in view of the Statue of Liberty. Just as well so the animals there couldn't sneak up on her. And there was Gracey, beautiful and blind. A little bit crazy, but as good as you could get.

Rook thought about it all the way out to the Rikers Island Bridge. How somebody was using her up to help their own cunty political careers: "The cop killer's locked up." And that Detective Dwight was dead and dirty. Dirty all the way back to Etillio and his gang. You start picking up that extra cash, you expect it, pretty soon you need it, you deserve it. Maybe his own twin brother was part of it way back when, which got Kirk dead, and then Etillio and the rest of them got the same from Kirk's twin brother. Poetic something or other, Sid would call it.

Kirk was his own flesh and had gone through the Academy with him, and rode the same cruiser before they got their gold shields on the same day. Then they sort of went their separate ways until Kirk got shot down like a dog in front of the Sephora Club by Etillio, who got what he had coming to him with all his jitbag mob fucks.

Then you got a dirtbag nigger cop putting three into you, so maybe there is and maybe there isn't reason to believe what he's telling you about your brother is anything but a bag of shit. But either way, it's a bag of shit now, with blind Grace Savoy in it.

Rook was all business when he got to Rikers Island. You're around the human garbage, you have to be. Inside he found that Bobby Perez had put him on the lawyer's list. Not a place he'd usually be caught dead on, but at Rikers it means no waiting unless they're counting heads.

Like he figured, she was in the North Infirmary. You put her anywhere near gen pop she's going to get eaten alive in ten minutes. The Mental Health Program was run by the Correctional Health Services of the New York City Department of Health. There were social workers, a psychiatrist, and lots of tranquilizers.

The social worker's name was Tillis. Short, stocky, wire glasses, and nicotine stains on his fingers and moustache. And that "I really don't give a damn" attitude that you have to have to keep from being played like a cheap violin.

"Ms. Savoy is sleeping," he said.

"Probably from all the late night parties she's been throwing."

"Excuse me," said Tillis.

"Wake her up."

"Pardon me?"

Rook moved in close enough to make any grown man on Thorazene nervous.

"Pardon me? Next you're going to say 'Fuck me.' I said wake her up. Unless of course, you got her all drugged so you can do what you want to and she's not going to complain."

Tillis started to get up from his desk. "I think I should get my supervisor."

Rook put his hand on the social worker's shoulder. "I think you should take me to see Grace Savoy before anybody's had a chance to cover anything up. I'll say hello, see she's alright. Then you can go catch a smoke. That would be nice. The alternative won't be. I promise you that. You understand?"

"Okay," said Tillis.

They went back to Gracey's room, passing through the universe of skel and crazy that was everywhere. She was standing at the door.

"Give me two of your smokes and your lighter," Lucas said.

The social worker complied.

"Now you know what a fish feels like," Rook told him. "Go somewhere and thank God you can sleep home tonight."

Tillis let Lucas in and left.

"Entirely rank rapist inside," said Gracey.

"Nobody's here but you," said Lucas.

"It's an anagram for Rikers Island Penitentiary, you know, scrambling the words around."

Rook gave her a cigarette and a light.

"Nosmo King," she said. "No smoking. That's another game. Like me being here." She took a deep drag.

"What kind of game is that, Gracey?"

She let her words come out in the exhale of the smoke. "I'm one of the 'MOPs.' Mental observation patients."

"You're in jail, Grace."

"They do have this lovely thing. The BOSS chair. Body Orifice Scanning System. You sit down and an alarm goes off if you got anything hidden up inside of you. I also hear they have these stun shields that give you 50,000 volts of electricity. More fun than Disneyland."

"A little reality here, Gracey. I got to know what's going on so I can do something about it. Your so-called lawyer said you're here is your doing."

She moved back against the sink and flicked an ash.

"So you think I should be at Elmhurst or King's County or the prison ward at Bellevue or Saint Vincent's?" She took another drag. "I say no thank you, sir. I am not a loony tune."

"So Spritzer's halfway right?"

"Precisely. The temporary order for observation had expired. The court, some fat colored lady, from what I could tell, issued an order to examine me for competency. To see whether I was loco, crazy, a bag of nuts. I told Russell to oppose it."

"To oppose it, Gracey?"

"Exactly, I'm tired of all that. People think because I'm artsy, I'm crazy, or I'm crazy because I'm blind, or I'm crazy because

I'm so beautiful. Well, I've been told a million times my whole life I'm crazy, which I am done with. So if they want me to be examined by their low-rent, court appointed shrinks, then they're the ones who are crazy."

"You sure about this, Gracey?"

"As sure as I am as to what happened on the roof. He shot you, my dear neighbor man, and he wanted to shoot me."

"You need somebody who can handle this, Grace. And that's not Russell what's-his-name, who does dog bite cases and whatnot. I'm getting you Warren Phelps. He's the best there is, which is what you got to have now."

"Of course, Lucas Rook, if he'll defend me like I deserve. Now you run along home and make sure my plants are alright."

"I'm serious, Gracey. You want Warren Phelps or not? He's expensive, but he's the best."

"Warren Phelps," she said.

"Good," Lucas said. "You need anything?"

"A carton of Kools would be nice. I would be rich as the King of Siam with that in here."

She lit her second cigarette and Rook drove back across the Rikers Bridge to where only half the folks were crud.

11

Lucas Rook drove to his office at 166 Fifth Avenue. No parking on the street, which meant paying ransom to the illegals at the garage. The usual group was smoking outside his office building. The douche bag printer came up to offer a discount on some mailer announcing that he was back to work.

"Maybe something like 'You can't keep a good man down,' " he said.

"I bet I could," said the pig-tailed girl lighting up her second Marlboro.

Manny's kid was in the foyer cleaning the glass on the tenant's directory. "Let me ride you up," he said.

"You're doing okay?" Rook asked him.

"Time goes by when you forget about it, Dad says. And he met some interesting people. Even a lawyer who used to be a tenant here. He'll be alright. He told me to tell you he was praying for you. I send him the newspapers."

The kid got out and went ahead and opened the office door.

"It looks nice," Rook told him. "I wouldn't have recognized it without the pizza boxes and Styrofoam cups and what not."

"I've got all your mail downstairs."

"Appreciate it."

The phone rang. It was Lieutenant Jaluski from IAB.

"I'll go get it," said Manny's kid.

Rook sat down and put his feet up on the desk. A little bonus that getting his chest shot up put a crimp in his workouts, which meant the bad leg from Etillio's beating was saying hello pretty regularly.

"You want something?" Rook said. "Because I got nothing for you."

"I know the blind girl's a friend of yours is at Rikers and you had something going on with Detective Graves."

"She's blind and he's dead, so you're looking for me to do what, which doesn't matter since I got nothing for you."

"They're looking at charging your girlfriend with Murder One."

The lieutenant waited for Rook to give something back, but it didn't happen.

"Maybe I got something for you, Rook," he tried.

"You want me to say 'About what, Jaluski?' Best you're going to get is for me to tell you to go stuff it where the sun don't shine."

"About your brother, Lucas."

"Go fuck yourself, Jaluski," said Rook as he hung up.

One of the charms of police work. You're sitting with nothing, you still make your play, lie, threaten, whatever. They open their mouths, you got them. They whine, they cry, they lie. They're giving you something.

Lucas checked his answering machine. Maybe a call that he'd won the lottery or whatever. The messages were mostly shit. Automated invitations for things he didn't want. Reminders to go to the dentist which could wait for a month or six. Somebody from the police retirees, and Shirl Freelang to say thank you for sending her to see Warren G. Phelps Esquire, who had saved her life.

Rook was dialing Phelps when Manny's son came in with the mail and a cup of coffee.

"Manny taught you right. Hang in there, kid. He can handle it."

"My dad says he'll be out before New Year's."

"Your dad's a good guy. It'll all be behind you before you notice."

The kid left. It'll never be behind either one of them. You're in the joint, you got that look lasts a year or so, but the nerves, they're shot and your kid's wondering the rest of his life if it's in the genes or whatever and he's going to wind up behind bars himself.

Lucas divided the mail into piles, a luxury not present when his desk was the way it was going to be in two or three days.

One of the piles went into the trash can. Advertisements, circulars, maybe they should get together, miracle hair growth, a hundred piece wrench set, your trip to sunny Antigua. The magazines not worth reading went next. Thank God for *Shotgun News*. The subscription to *Nipples* was probably expired. Next in the circular file went the bills marked "Friendly Reminder." It's friendly, it's bullshit.

The medical bills and statements from the insurance companies went into a folder. Medical billing was artful thieving. If you're big enough you do it so it looks like you're entitled to ask for three times more than you should. Plus you put your lying in code so nobody knows what you're talking about anyway. Right now none of this shit was his responsibility, but he put a rubber band around the folder and dropped it into the bottom drawer of the filing cabinet in case he went ahead to sue somebody for what happened on the roof.

The last pile wasn't bullshit. A note in black fountain pen ink from Catherine Wren's father. Thick stationery with some embossed something on the envelope. "We have met, but only once. However, I know that my daughter, Catherine, holds you most dear. If I can be of any assistance in your time of need, feel free to contact me at my private number above." Ballsy thing for a highbrow type in his 80s.

Rook opened the letter from Circuit City last. A referral from Dick Warden he had worked the D'Angelo-Westie job for and then had gotten him a Pasadena he's buying the pussy of a fifteen-year-old. The Circuit City letter was a confidential request for his services to resolve an old con game with a new twist. You got one of your employees making false merch returns which they turn into the gift cards and then into cash. If that panned out, and the thing for Owls, money would be okay for a while.

Lucas went over to his couch that was décor when he had a waiting room. The endurance was coming slow, but not the bullshit. Gracey needed help, he needed to keep his apartment, and Jaluski needed his ass handed to him for talking about Kirk. Right now he needed to stretch out.

Fuck Frank Jaluski and fuck Dwight Graves. No way was Kirk a dirty cop. Kirk didn't have anybody on the side. No family problems that meant big bills. No big home. He didn't gamble or have a drinking problem, so it didn't make sense. You're his twin brother, you know what he's made of.

Rook fell asleep quickly and the dream came just as fast. He was working up an alley. Two skels had their eyes on him. It was dark, but he could see everything as if there were big strobe lights or something. Kirk was in the alley, too. He was up ahead and Lucas could tell that he had the answers to all the questions.

Lucas went after his twin brother, walking fast. Now breaking into a run. His heart was pounding which scared him like he was going to have a heart attack, but he kept at it, closing the distance so they were quickly side by side, Lucas Rook wanting answers from his brother and to get those skels in the dark. Then the bad guys came together like there was only one of them and then so did Kirk and Lucas Rook and then the two of them were both shadows which came together and then broke apart.

Lucas awoke in a sweat. He got up slow and washed his face. Then he poured himself a Jack and drank it down. His heart slowed. He looked at the clock and placed a call to Warren G. Phelps. The master lawyer was in court, but would call when he returned.

He called the risk manager at Circuit City about the letter Warden had sent. The guy's name was Scott. The job was waiting. They set up an appointment. The money was good, and the healing holes in his chest wouldn't be at risk. Then Lucas called his friends over at Rikers to remind them to keep their eyes on Grace Savoy.

Rook put his vest back on with the plate over his heart and got his guns to go outside and walk over a couple of blocks for a bowl of chili and a beer.

The phone rang again. It was Gransback, who had come knocking to discuss something about how concerned the building management was about what happened on the roof.

"I'm on my way to see my lawyer about how we're going to sue your sorry asses and I'm going to own this place," Rook told him.

"Oh my," said the real estate man.

"Don't worry, I'm thinking about keeping you on here. You are so fucking polite."

12

Warren G. Phelps Esquire, barrister and magician, did not return Rook's call until after nine that night, by which time the evening's combination of pain meds and beer had given Lucas a decent buzz.

"Thought maybe you had forgot," he told Phelps.

"I'm just finishing dinner, Lucas. You know by now that I return calls."

"Right, Counselor. The 'G' stands for good guy."

Phelps lit a cigar, turning it in slow circles in just above the flame. "Everything alright?"

Rook opened another cold one. "Except me being shot and my friend's in Rikers that saved my sorry ass."

"The blind girl, your neighbor. I read about it in *The Times*."

"The grapevine's talking they're charging Murder One."

Another call came in on the attorney's cell. He let it go. "That's not sensible for the State to do, Lucas, but possible."

"She can pay, Warren. How much?"

"I'll discuss that with her. My secretary will call you for the particulars. I know I should get a Blackberry, but a man has to have time to enjoy a good cigar and talk to his friends. You on the mend?"

"Sure, sure. I appreciate it, Warren. I'll make you a home-cooked meal, bake you a cake."

"I'll speak to you tomorrow afternoon after I've gotten in to see her. The name's Savoy if I recall, like the old hotel."

"Grace Savoy. She's at Rikers. I'll let them know you're on it."

"My people will take care of that, Lucas."

So will mine, thought Rook, but he let it go. "Tomorrow, Counselor, first thing. You'll be on the list."

"Excellent, Lucas. I got to take this call," said Phelps and he hung up.

So at least he was up and rolling, the new thing at Circuit City, the job with Owls, and helping Gracey out. Lucas tried some light shadow boxing, which hurt. He settled on cleaning his new Glocks and going over in his mind for the thousandth time how things would be different if he had shot Dwight Graves first.

Rook stayed up watching television and trying not to think. At least not over and over and over. Fuck that post-traumatic shit. Maybe a painkiller and one more beer would stop that shit. Then again, maybe mixing alcohol with the meds could stop him altogether. That would be a surprise, but so was you just got shot, your blind friend is in Rikers facing a world of shit because she saved your life that you couldn't, and IAB's talking about your brother.

All this bullshit running crazy in your head while you're awake which was another flavor of the shit of when he was asleep. That crazy shit he was used to since Kirk got blown away and he got to see what looked just like him with his blood running into the gutter. This new pity party was something Dr. DiBona had warned him about, post traumatic whatever.

Lucas took one of the nutsy pills Dr. DiBona had given him and fell asleep into his dreaming freak show. Different from his daytime freak show only in that half the shit made no sense whatsoever, like him and Kirk driving around in one of those kid's fire engines you pedal and then him parking it and not being able to find it and they're both bleeding from holes that were like the eyes that murdering fuck, Delbert Fine, had tattooed all over his crazy body a couple of years back in Philly. Then the Lorazepam kicked in and his brain stopped yelling at him.

The answering machine in the front room was flashing when Lucas finally got up. A call from Phelps' office that he was meeting with Grace Savoy at 10 AM and a call from Valerie Moon, could she come over and rock his world, gently.

Lucas picked up his messages from his office. A robot call to buy resort land in the Poconos. The other call was from Gilligan. The lovebirds in Jersey had just checked in to the beautiful Englewood Motel.

Rook thought about going over to Joe Oren's to grab a cup of coffee and maybe a ride out to finish the job for Owls Miksis. Fuck it. He called over to the garage so his Mercury would be up front and made himself a cup of instant. The Westside Highway, I95, Route 4 to catch the two lovebirds doing it doggie style, except it was the lovely missus delivering it with a strap-on.

Lucas was in the door and took some close-ups, which got him horrified face shots, and then one of them trying to cover up the dildo that a few moments ago had been part of them.

"*Vice* Principal is right," Rook said as he flashed his badge. Then he drove to Slavitt's to get a chopped sirloin platter and a couple of cold ones. His chest hurt, but his head felt good.

You're doing a peeper job leaves a bad taste even after a well-seasoned strip steak and two bourbons. The good piece of peach pie and coffee took care of that.

Lucas paid cash. You put this meal on plastic's going to make it not so easy to deny you were at the Englewood Motel if something gets screwed up. He went to the motel and picked up the lamp with the video camera inside. He was out on the highway when the chances of that screw-up increased about a hundred times.

It was the catcher from the afternoon delight at the motel. The asshole was driving up close from behind, which made some sense the way he was handling his love life.

Rook hit the brakes hard, which put the Pontiac behind him into a swerve. Another fancy maneuver from the good old days had lover boy looking at Rook in his rearview. Lover boy sped up. Lucas let him go at first, then punched it after him. This was good stuff.

You're a cop forever in the time that you still can put on a show. Rook drove alongside and pointed to pull it over. Let him think he's got even bigger problems that he ever thought about when he got caught being the bitch in heat.

The guy was shaking when Lucas walked up to the parked Pontiac. The mope was reaching for the glove box, not a good thing in any scenario.

"Put your hands on the steering wheel," Rook told him.

"My registration…"

"And shut up."

"I…"

"You are begging for it, Mr. Lachman."

"You know my name."

"Of course I do. I know everything about you. Where you work, your wife. Sordid, absolutely sordid."

Lachman pissed himself.

"What can I do, what can I do?" he said.

"You? Probably nothing. Me, I can ruin your life."

"Please, please."

"I hate people who beg. Although that's your scene, 'lifestyle' as they say. I also hate people who ride up on my bumper."

"I was only trying to…"

"Do me grievous bodily harm." Good old police jargon.

"No, not that. To save my life from going down the drain." The man started to shake.

"Wouldn't want that to happen now, would we," said Rook. "Besides, pissing yourself and getting fucked in the ass should be enough for one day. So why don't you just drive safely now."

Rook went back to his Mercury and waited for the poor slob to pull away. Maybe if Lachman hadn't come up where he could get the tag number, he wouldn't have gotten the rough treatment.

Then again, maybe he would. And the mope probably liked it anyways.

Warren Phelps called for his limo after the bank confirmed that Grace Savoy's wire transfer had gone through. In criminal work you always made sure that your retainer cleared before you got involved. In the old days, getting out of the case was not difficult. "Your Honor, I regretfully must withdraw as defense counsel as Mr. Green has yet to arrive." Now to avoid being held in the case by the court as well as for simple economic reasons, smart lawyers, let alone brilliant ones, gave nothing more than an appointment without being paid.

For homicide cases, the usual Phelps retainer was fifty thousand dollars, reduced for this matter to forty as a professional courtesy to Rook. The fee went into Phelps' escrow account to be drawn out at the hourly rate of seven hundred fifty per hour. Pity be to the dumb slob lawyer who, needing the cash flow, puts the money into his operating account before actually doing the work. The only thing dumber than that was taking cash, even if it was to avoid the Feds scuttling your defense by claiming that your fee was ill-gotten gains and therefore subject to seizure.

Off to the cesspool that was Rikers Island. In the beginning, a million years ago, you got there early and hung around and hoped to pick up a new client there. Now the sounds and sights and smells of the street evil and the desperation were things Warren was glad were no longer part of his daily life.

Grace Savoy was waiting for him. She looked pale and boyish in her prison infirmary garb, but somehow all the more beautiful for it. "I'm ready to defend myself, Warren G. Phelps," she said.

"And how do you know who I am?"

"Is this some insensitive quiz show game?" she asked. "*Deal or No Deal?* Well, I already told them no deal."

Phelps sat down. "Did someone offer you a deal?"

"No deal. No suitcase with a million dollars for my freedom. And this is not some quiz show game, *Truth or Consequences*."

"I'm just trying to get to know you, Ms. Savoy."

Phelps made a note and asked the question again. "How do you know who I am? It's a question."

Grace sniffed the air. "The smell of an expensive suit, a starched shirt. Lilac aftershave and the aroma of a good cigar. The sound of your briefcase against your side. Also, they told me it was you."

"I'd like to go over some ground rules first, Ms. Savoy. I work for you. I acknowledge that. But you will do exactly as I say. If we disagree, I will be happy to discuss any matter with you, but if you insist on disregarding my directions, I will withdraw as your attorney. The unused part of your retainer will be returned."

"Chill," Grace said, "whilst I bust me down with an ace." She balled her hands into fists. "You're abandoning me. Leaving me high and dry. High and dry and blind. I'm blind. I'm beautiful. And I shot that black fucker dead."

"I am not abandoning you, Ms. Savoy. And you are never to repeat that last remark. Do you understand me?"

She lit a cigarette, then cupped the smoke at her side. "I'm okay," she said. "Let's begin. I won't say that last thing again."

"No racial epithets either, Ms. Savoy. Black fucker or so forth."

"No jungle bunny, spade, porchmonkey, jigaboo."

"Exactly."

She took a deep drag of menthol smoke and spoke though her exhale. "I got rules myself, Mr. Phelps. No insanity defense."

Phelps made another note. "I usually reserve trial strategy for myself or someone with at least as much trial experience and success as I have."

"Lucas told me you were the best, and I believe he is correct. As correct as I was in blowing away that jitbag cocksucker who shot him, which is the last time I say that. I do solemnly swear."

"Rule number two, Gracey."

"Somebody as pretty as I am says jitbag, it's a shock. I know that."

"Actually, jitbag's one of my favorite words. There's *melody*, *foreswore*, and *jitbag*. They're all my favorites. It's that you will not say what happened on that roof unless I have told you that it's okay to say what happened on that roof and that we agree on exactly how you are going to say it. You've violated that rule for the very last time or I shall not represent you. Do you understand and agree?"

She took another pull on her menthol. "Okie-dokie."

"Then we have a deal, which is you will speak about what happened on the roof only as we agree and you will refrain from using racial slurs until I tell you that you may resume if you so desire. I will defend you with all my skills up to the moment it appears that there is a strong possibility that we are in conflict as to whether and how we are to use your mental state as a defense strategy by a 703.30, 40.15 or similar defense. That is the only caveat."

"He had problems too. Manic depression or something."

"Who's that, Grace?"

"Dick Caveat. The Yale boy with the talk show on television."

"Right, Gracey."

"You're smiling, Warren G. Phelps. Lucas told me to remember the 'G.' I can tell from your voice you're smiling."

"They're going to be moving you, Grace. Where to is important."

"No way I bitch in," she said.

"I appreciate your quick mastery of the jailhouse patois, but this is important," her lawyer said. "It will tell us how unreasonable they're going to be. If they transfer you to Bedford Hills means that."

"I was hoping for Beacon, counselor."

"That's not going to happen with a dead cop." He looked at his watch. "Glenn Goord's gone at DOC, but I'm reasonably sure we can get you in Bayview, which is at 20th and 12th Avenue. After *you be chainin', it's bam-bam for sho for dis limbo, so don't you be frettin' 'bout no daggin or gassin'."*

"I appreciate that, Warren. It's the *elbow* I'm worried about."

"A life sentence is as unlikely as the death penalty, Grace."

"I appreciate that," she said. "One more thing."

"And what's that?"

"My pussy jewelry. They confiscated that when they brought me here."

"You want me to say 'I'll look into that' or something similar. I'm not going to say that, Gracey. If you need me, I'm just a phone call away."

Attorney Phelps enjoyed his Cohiba on the way back to his office. What was on his mind was the rest of the day and his fine Cuban cigar, which he enjoyed without the distraction of his cell phone and the Blackberry which he refused to use.

His office at Lexington Avenue was a good arrangement. Most of his floor was a patent firm, IP, Intellectual Property, they called it now. Friedman, who shared space on the floor above, was getting off the elevator as he got in. He tipped his derby hat. "Good to see you, Warren. I may have someone for you. Tax issues."

"We can chat over lunch, Phillip."

Phelps picked up his messages from his receptionist, a tall woman in a green suit. Three from Grace Savoy, either an emergency or hysterics, understandable under the circumstances. Then again, maybe she was crazy. Also the client who had mistaken lobbying for laundering, to say he was going to be twenty minutes late.

Warren turned on his computer, a reminder to bill Shirl Freelang for follow-up to his genius on her cigarette tax problem. Also a reminder of his yearly check-up with Dr. Ehrlich, the dermatologist.

He dictated his memo of the meeting with Grace Savoy and called the DA to start his magic act. It would be quite a show, the blind beauty to the rescue and the two men shot, one the black detective and the other one Lucas Rook.

13

Valerie Moon called from downstairs.

"I'm here, Lucas. I've come to keep you warm."

The place was a mess, but she had other things on her mind. He buzzed her up.

Valerie had her hair down and was wearing a fur coat. "You like?" she said.

"I don't know if I'm ready for this."

"The coat I mean. About the other, now don't you worry, I'll take care of everything. And I do have clothes on under this."

She opened her fur to show her nurse's uniform.

Valerie put her hand on Rook's chest. He was wearing his bulletproof vest under his sweat shirt. "Are you alright, honey?"

"You're the only person in the world who can call me that, you know."

She sat down on the couch and patted the cushion for him to join her. "I know that, dear. Now just sit and down and rest." Valerie pretended to be reading a piece of paper. "Now the doctor was specific. No generic substitutes permitted. I am absolutely to check your lovely boys."

Valerie Moon could show up in a nurse's outfit, give you a blow-job and make you feel like you were doing her a favor. She got up and went into the kitchen. "I'll bring us some beers, okay?"

"Sure, sure," he said.

She came back with two Coors Lite.

"And she drinks her beer from the can. What more could a fellow ask for."

"I have an interview today, Mr. Rook. You will be proud of me. Leaving the world of culinary service behind and entering the world of the professionals." She popped the can open. "Cheers."

Lucas joined her. "Nothing to do with liars, I mean lawyers, I hope."

"I have my integrity." She adjusted the collar on her white blouse. "I am going to be the office manager for a doctor."

"And therefore the nurse's outfit. I thought that was special for me. And you know how much about the field? A friend of yours, I assume."

"Actually, yes." She took another sip. "But hand jobs only." She started to laugh. "That's a joke." Valerie leaned over and kissed him on the cheek. "We do have good times, don't we, Mr. Lucas Rook?"

"We do, Ms. Valerie Moon." He looked at his watch. "I've got to go see my surgeon. We can share a cab."

"Deal," she said. "Now just give me a second. Beer makes this nurse have to go pee. And then you must sit absolutely still while I give you some head you will never forget."

Valerie and Lucas went out to get a taxi. Rook never took the first cab. It took three more until he flagged down one driven by a small white man chewing on an unlit cigar.

Lucas got out at the doctor's office and gave the driver a twenty. "Treat her right," he told the old man. "I got your medallion number."

Dr. DiBona's waiting room was jammed with middle-aged men trying not to look scared.

Lucas went up to the check-in desk.

"We're running behind," said the not Valerie Moon with the black glasses.

"I can reschedule," said Rook.

"Name," she whispered.

Rook leaned in. "Why the secrecy?"

"HIPAA," she said. "Name."

"Lucas Rook," he whispered. "How long?"

"At least another hour."

"By which you mean two."

"Doctor had an emergency."

Lucas asked for the men's room key. You get shot in the chest you don't skip your appointment the way you do the dentist, but no way could he sit anywhere for two hours. Those days of sitting in his unmarked for a shift were over. Drain his vein, read the paper. Maybe go out for a while until Dr. B showed.

Rook was going back into DiBona's office when the doc got off the elevator.

"I'll be with you as soon as I can," he said.

"Your receptionist said an hour."

"Give me fifteen minutes, Detective. I'll take care of it, otherwise it will be the hour and a half you suspected."

"Two."

"Most likely," said DiBona as he went into his office through the back door.

Twenty-five minutes later Rook was called to the front desk and sent to a room.

A nurse came in, jet black hair, blue eyes, a hottie, except that she had a piece of chewing gum stashed in the side of her mouth. 70-30 she had a tattoo running down her ass, "tramp stamp" they called it. She took Rook's BP and weighed him, Glock, back-up piece and Second Chance Kevlar included.

Then she told him to remove his clothes to the waist like she didn't give a shit. A tech who looked exactly like Doogie Howser came in.

"I'm not him and I'm not gay," the EKG technician said.

"Okay," said Lucas as he lay down.

"NPH, a fag? I don't believe it." Doogie put on the little suction cups, ran the heart test, and then took the electric leads back off again.

"Down the hall, second door to the right."

"Swell," said Rook. He put his V neck sweatshirt and his hardware back on and went to the treatment room.

"Back to work, I see," said DiBona when he came in.

"I'm good, Doc."

"I'd prefer you not get into another shootout for a bit, whether you're wearing a vest or not."

"That's not high on my list of things I got planned to do. Right. Get decent seats for the next home game, buy yourself a new watch, take three in the chest."

Dr. DiBona sat down and gestured for Rook to take off his shirt.

"Wounds look good. Any seepage?"

"Came and went."

"You starting to move up the exercises a bit? Brisk walking is good. Nothing, pardon my word, 'explosive' yet. No weight lifting. Like that."

"Like hitting the bag?"

"Like that. Your appetite okay?"

"No problem."

"Good," said Dr. DiBona. "If you're not having sex, you should. It's good for you. You need it, I'll write her a prescription."

"I'm good."

"PTSD, Post Traumatic Stress Disorder, is a normal result of what you've been through," the doctor went on. "From mild forgetfulness to depression, paranoia. The meds I gave you will help or you can see somebody."

"I'm getting back to normal, whatever that is."

"I hear you, but take it easy."

Rook put his vest back on. "Appreciate it, Doc. This here's a fashion statement."

"I'll see you in four weeks. You have any problems, call me."

Lucas passed the EKG tech on the way out.

"Homo for sure, Neil Patrick Harris. No doubt," Lucas told him.

Rook walked a half-dozen blocks slow and then cabbed over to Jimbo Turner's stand. The shineman was working on a pair of brown and whites when Lucas came up.

Jimbo turned around. "Well, it's a good day, a good day," he said. "You sit on down. Shine's on me."

Rook started up on to the stand, but a pain from the incision got to him. The shineman offered his shoulder as a boost, but Lucas ignored him and pulled himself up.

"How ya doin', Jimbo?"

"Not bad for a half-blind, diabetic white shineman. Glad to see you're up and around."

He washed the shoes and rubbed a coat of saddlesoap in with his hand. Then he took a piece of nylon stocking from his drawer and tied it around his pointer finger to put in some color. "Darken them up now that the season changed," he said.

Then the brushes clickety-clack, clickety-clack, and the rag snapping like a starched sail in the ocean's wind. Jimbo took his bottle of his special oil out and applied two drops.

"You out here to get your shoes like glass, you got to be okay, Lucas Rook."

"I'm good, Jimbo Turner."

Rook got himself down using the shineman's shoulder.

"I wanted to come by and see my good friend," Lucas said.

"I appreciate that, Mr. Rook. I surely do."

"As much as them Jersey tomatoes, Mr. Turner?"

"A little more, I think." Jimbo Turner smiled, the only one Lucas had seen in all those years.

Rook walked a couple of blocks again. The cane he used when the old injury flared up would have made it a lot easier to move, but he wasn't what he was before Dwight Graves shot him up on the roof. His strength wasn't back or even his anger. And if you're walking with a cane, you're waiting for somebody to take a bite out of you.

There was a saloon across the street and Lucas Rook went inside to have a Jack and a draft chaser.

"I know you," said the ugly man at the other end of the bar. Big and ugly walking over. He had his beer mug in his hand. The kind of hunk of glass you could cut somebody up with bad if they couldn't handle themselves.

"You locked me up once," he said.

Lucas reached down with his right hand to his back-up piece. Two more steps and ugly's going to be looking down the barrel of something that would erase him.

"You changed my life, you surely did," said the big man. He put his beer mug down and reached out his hand.

Rook nodded, but did not remove his hand from this ankle piece.

"I got his tab," said the ugly man.

"I'm one and done," said Lucas Rook.

"Then one it is."

The bartender turned around and poured another Jack Daniels. Lucas drank his bourbon down and left two singles on the bar. He watched the ugly man in the mirror as he went out.

14

Lucas Rook thought about going up to his office. Open the mail, pick up his messages, but his apartment won out. And maybe not the "apartment" much longer. The management of the St. Claire, the owners, the REIT, whoever the fuck, could be persuaded they wanted to settle any claims he might be thinking about, clear the balance sheet so they could get their conversion through. Not get the blood off the place, those type of people never even saw that kind of shit. To them, it was ten thousand miles away.

He stopped at the garage on the way back to stretch out on the sofa. Sid Rosen was at his desk with his glasses up on his head and talking to himself.

"I interrupt something, Sidney?"

"Reading Shakespeare to Bear here. He likes it like the other Bear did."

"Your dogs like *Hamlet* or whatever?"

"Actually, it's *Macbeth*, but you got to read it out loud is the only way."

Rook sat down and stretched his legs. "Especially that part, 'out damned spot' if he goes on the rug."

"Very good, Lucas boy. That deserves a drink."

The bourbon he'd had at the saloon was wearing off, so it was not a bad idea. "For medicinal purposes, Sid."

Rosen poured them each a drink.

"Good to see you up and around," he said. "Funny thing how quick you can see the world deconstruct."

"Philosophy, right?"

"Eyesight. You're looking at a building an' all of a sudden you're seeing just the bricks. You don't get busy or have a drink, you're seeing the individual bricks, one by one."

Rook finished his drink. The German shepherd came over and sniffed him good.

"He can still smell the hospital on you."

Or the blood, Rook thought. "I'm making a Last Will and Testament, Sid, now that I almost cashed out. I *bequeath*, that's a Shakespeare word, all the books of yours I haven't given back to you."

"And my will gives all I got to my partner here," said Rosen. "Ain't that right, Bear? Or my old lady, if she's still alive and Bear don't want my stuff." He filled his glass a second time, but Lucas waved him off. "We're all just an MRI away, Lucas boy."

Rook got up to go. "Appreciate your being at the hospital, Sidney."

"I know you do." The garageman slid his glasses back on his head and began reading again to his dog.

Lucas went around to Joe Oren's. They all were there. Sam was frying up some okra in the back. Joe was calling his bread order in, and Jeanie was doing homework at the counter.

"Well, here he is," said Joe. "Back again."

Jeanie kissed Lucas on the cheek. Sam came out from the back.

"Well, you sit down and let Samuel feed you right."

"We all could eat," said Joe.

"Like a party, or Thanksgiving," Jeanie said.

Rook was hungry from the drinking and it was like the good dreams he didn't have, but he wondered how his stomach would do. I'll go slow, he told himself. It don't get too much better than this. A thought about Catherine Wren came into his head. Then Tuze, who was lying in the nursing home.

Jeanie brought over a cup of coffee and a piece of pie.

"I made this lemon meringue myself," she said.

Nobody bothered to confirm that it was the usual lie.

"Don't you be filling up yourself, Lucas Rook," said Sam. "We got a meal to eat. And the cobbler afterwards."

"I could do two desserts. Starting with this first one made by my Jeanie girl."

Rook's cell phone rang. It was Grace Savoy.

"They beat me up. They beat me up," she said.

"You alright, Gracey?" Rook went across the room.

"They hurt my face. And then they tried to grab my junk. But when they got in close I hurt them bad. Blind Russell taught me how to fight."

"Who's they?"

"Two of my fellow guests."

"Are you in segregation now?"

"I'm in the infirmary. They didn't hurt my face."

"I'll take care of this, Gracey. I got this."

Rook called Bobby Perez on his cell and told him what happened.

"I am out, Rook. My sister had her wisdom teeth pulled. She don't have nobody. The new man transferred in. I told him."

"She got hurt, Bobby. I was counting on you."

"I'm sorry. What can I say to you? It won't go down again. I give you my word."

"You can tell me you got two sisters now. One of them's named Grace."

Lucas could hear Perez light up a smoke. Bobby Perez took a deep inhale and spoke through the smoke coming out. "I got two sisters now, Rook."

"I'm coming to pay a visit, Bobby. Meanwhile, I need you to get back to the Rock and call me and put Grace on the phone so I know you're standing next to her."

"Done," said Perez and he hung up.

Lucas Rook had that look when he turned around.

Jeanie started to cry, but wasn't sure why. "I didn't make the pie," she said. "The delivery man bought it. I mean brought it. Daddy bought it."

Her father wiped his freckled face on his apron.

"Why don't you help Sam get the dinner ready, honey?" he said.

The cook neither needed or wanted help, but he knew what was going on. "About time I show you a secret or two about my dirty rice."

You work the streets, you handle two, three things at a time easy. You talk to somebody while you're listening to another conversation across from you. Like Ray Tuzio told him when he was just a young pup. You better be using your rear view and both side mirrors when you're sitting down to take a crap.

Lucas Rook ate the chicken stew and biscuits with the dirty rice like he was enjoying it big time while he was waiting for Bobby Perez to call that everything was alright and deciding to call Warren Phelps and whether to do that now or tomorrow morning. And also making alternative plans if Bobby didn't hold up his end and what he was going to do to the pus bags who put a hurting on Gracey.

Rook was getting ready to go out to Rikers when the call came through.

"I got her," Perez said. "It's not bad. Nothing permanent. Mostly scared is all."

"She got any marks on her face, Bobby?"

"A shiner maybe. And a bruise on her chin. Nothing."

"It better not be. Let me talk to her."

Gracey got on the phone. "I don't know what to do," she said. "Maybe there'll be more of them."

"No there won't," said Rook.

"Maybe they're that black cop's friends. The one I, you know." She changed her voice to hip-hop, "Goin' to cap my ass. Going to step to."

"Put him on the phone again," Lucas said.

"She's alright, Rook. I got this."

"Tell her she has your word."

"You know, Rook…"

"Tell her."

Bobby Perez did it, then Grace got on the phone.

"He told me that I will be alright, neighbor. He gave me his word. Said I was his little sister now. But you're coming to my rescue, aren't you, Lucas?"

"Of course I am."

"I'm blind, you know," said Gracey.

"I'm coming out to see you."

"Now?" said Grace Savoy.

"Soon. I will tuck you in."

"I'll say that you told him to let me smoke cigarettes. 'Drag the ace,' they say up in here. Nighty night."

Joe Oren gave Rook the 'Do you need anything?' look.

"Was that work?" Jeanie asked Lucas.

"Routine, Jeanie. Everything's fine."

"Sounded like you were talking to a girl."

"Help me with these dishes," Sam told her.

"Going to roll, people," said Lucas Rook. "Appreciate the fine meal and the company."

"You're going to rescue a damsel in distress. I'm a damsel."

"And we're the Three Musketeers, your Dad, Sam, and me."

Lucas went out the back door and through the alley. He went out there now, there was nothing he could do. Perez was good for it, and it was more important that Warren Phelps would start a shitstorm. He'd be out there to punctuate it after the Circuit City meeting he had set up.

Lucas stopped for a quart of fresh squeezed orange juice and a *Daily News* on the block before the St. Claire. As he came up on the building he saw an unmarked pull away. The driver inside looked like Antopol, who really had no good reason for being there now.

Rook went into his building. The assistant manager came out to offer an extra friendly help. Way extra friendly because he never said hello before at all. Good things can happen when you have somebody by the throat. With the credit in the bank for bringing in Grace's case, he could get Warren Phelps to handle muscling the St. Claire people into buying him off. Best deal would be I'll pay you what I'm paying you as a condo fee or whatever and the place is mine. Worst is they roll the price back, maybe finance the deal at cost. Nothing like that was happening without fancy lawyering.

The orange juice gave him acid stomach. Lucas popped some Tums upstairs and waited for his insides to settle down while he ran though the channels. He fell asleep for an hour until Grace called.

"They put me in administrative segregation," she said. " 'Ad Seg,' they call it. I'm snug as a bug in a rug. Your friend, Mr. Perez, came by to see me twice."

"That's nice, Gracey."

"You sleeping, neighbor?" she asked.

"Not now," he told her.

"I want to come home."

"Mr. Phelps is a fine attorney," Rook said.

"He said I'll be out of here soon," Gracey said. "I called him. He called me back."

"Warren's a good man."

"You too, Lucas Rook," said Grace Savoy. "I wish you were here."

15

Now that he knew that Gracey was alright, Lucas called over to Phelps to get him on it. Then he got up and went out to make some money. He called over to the garage that he was going out so Sid could move his car out front.

"You want company?" Rosen asked. "Me and Bear here could use a change of scenery."

"Meeting a client in Brooklyn."

"Could be our fourth largest city, Lucas boy, were it not one of the boroughs. 'Home to Everyone from Everywhere' is the motto."

Rook took the keys off the board.

"Did I tell you, I saw Sandy Amoros' catch and throw?"

"No you did not, Sidney."

"That should be 'The Catch,' not Willie's off of Vic Wertz. Then the cocksuckers move out to LA in two years. That should've been the Battle of Brooklyn."

"Which you'll edify me about when I get back," said Rook.

Even with his vest and its titanium shield over his heart, Lucas drove with the seat all the way back so that the airbag didn't send him back to the hospital. One of the last cases he worked for the PD, lovely neighborhood lady's giving some shine deep throat, he runs into the back of a Toyota. The airbag deploys, she's got a broken neck and a helluva explanation to give if she wasn't dead, Rastus winds up in surgery so he only has an anaconda when they're done.

Circuit City could be a decent client. A corporation that size would have a decent Loss Prevention Department. But once the shitbags were off of the premises, it was either the PD or private and PD got their hands full to do anything but drive by the parking lot on the weekends.

Mr. Scott was not there for their meeting at the store. His assistant, Raja Searles, reddish hair and freckles which you saw every now and then on a Tyronne, knew how to explain how they were getting banged on a return scam. Lucas takes out his notebook for show and gets Searles going. "Customer comes in, buys a set of decent cables, maybe a boxed CD set and runs a duplicate of the receipt off of his computer. Then he lifts a couple more of the items from store number two, and returns them all back here."

Rook nodded. "He's cutting the fence out doubles, triples his money."

"The fence?"

Like he didn't know what "fence" meant. "The middleman. He pays fifteen percent on the 'merch,' the merchandise, the goods, and passes it on in the stream of commerce. How long this been going on?"

Searles smoothed out his tie. "This is new. Mostly what we've been experiencing is through credit cards, so we have our credit card fraud units to handle that."

"You got surveillance tapes for me?"

"We do indeed. But you're a new vendor, so Mr. Scott says for me get you straightened out with Human Resources first. They handle all the incidental employment. That's what we call service contracts for one store only, or in this case, two."

Lucas closed his interview book. "You have decent surveillance, maybe we grab your thief before he undoes all the good publicity coming out of your Jersey employee turning in them Fort Dix terrorists."

"I do hope so," said Searles. "But no 'grabbing' at all, please. My instructions are for you to secure the information only. I'll get the tapes for you while you get registered with HR. In the meantime I'm going to take a cigarette, for which I have to go outside."

He got Rook on the phone with Human Resources, then gestured with his smoke on the way out. "Urban legend," he said. By which he either meant about cigarettes causing cancer or that blacks smoked menthols. Either way, who gave a flying fuck.

It took about a three cigarette break for Rook to get his temporary vendor clearance.

"You ready to go?" said Searles when he got back. "I've got enough tape to make a television series. You'll see them right off. White male, woman of color wearing a bhurka. My guess is you look at the surveillance at the Bayridge store, you'll see the white male making the returns."

"And my directions and parameters are specifically what? Or do I get that from Mr. Scott?"

"The woman who does the shoplifting here, we have her license place from our cameras that cover the parking lot. We obviously can't do anything with that ourselves. Once you secure her information and whatever else confirmation you can on her and her partner, we give that all to the police and they make the arrests. Mr. Scott told me to emphasize that you are to gather information only."

"No problem," Lucas told him. No problem whatsoever if you lay a television on the detective who takes your complaint. Otherwise it goes nowhere. But it will be just fine to charge by the hour, get paid mileage. First the video, then surveilling and so on. Everything's no problem when the meter's running.

The job was an opportunity to renew old acquaintances. Piechowski still running the 68th precinct like the old days. Not the *good* old days when they worked the two decap jobs at The Narrows. Maybe set up a meet with Mark Johnson, who was running cases at the Brooklyn DA. The only people who called it what it was, "The Kings County DA," were the same ones who called

Sixth Avenue "The Avenue of the Americas." Bam, the cost of your cab ride just tripled.

And for sure, the stop at Fort Hamilton, "The Army's Ambassador to New York City" and Art Blessing, the real deal, who ran the Criminal Investigation Command with a patch over one eye and a lovely lady as a CO. Turning that meeting into good billing would take some ingenuity, but all those years on the job you absolutely learn how to write a report.

Lucas went out to find a place that served a decent breakfast. Dunkin Donuts was good because of the coffee. Mickey D's wasn't for the same reason. The Arrow was perfect. The coffee strong and hot, scrambled eggs that were not runny, and grits with just enough butter that all of his docs would be flipping out.

The way The Arrow was set up, you could sit at the counter and still see the front door. And since they still honored Masterbadge, you'd have a cop or two in there regularly. A uniform came in for take-out, a rookie by the way he wasn't eyeballing the place, but he left a couple of singles for the cashier's pocket which meant somebody had schooled him decent.

Rook had the kind of breakfast that made you glad you were in the USA, home of pork roll and the like. He got change for the newspaper boxes out front and took three back to the Circuit City for while the tapes ran. Ten minutes into the show he sees her all wrapped up like a ninja or whatever, even with one of these face masks, which means the perp could be male, female, white, black, whatever. One of these days, somebody's going to let their good sense catch up with their concern for minority sensitivity and have the same kind of "no masks" rule everywhere like they have in banks.

There she is stuffing the shit under her robes. A little later on some white guy's talking to her up at the checkout. A second tape, she's back, a guy looks like whitey's with her in the parking lot, but they drive away in separate vehicles. The video gives you the tag for Mrs. Muslim, so you run that, check the owner through BCI and see what the address gives you.

After the *Post, Times,* and the *Brooklyn Daily Eagle*, it was time to have a little facetime with Raja.

"Going to check in with your other store," Rook told him. Searles was on his cell phone and answered with an 'OK' signal.

Okay all around. Lucas headed over to the Circuit City in Bayridge with a legit stopover at the 69th. The desk sergeant was an old-timer, Jimmy Kehoe.

"Well, look what the cat dragged in," the desk said. "Glad to see you're up and around. Helluva thing, helluva thing."

"I'm good, young man. Sonny upstairs? I'm working a return scam."

"Then Sonny's your man."

"King of the con games," Lucas said.

A Hassid came in. The desk sergeant pointed for him to move back.

"Stand behind the yellow line, Rabbi," he said. "I call them all Rabbi."

Lucas went upstairs to give Sonny what he had on the Circuit City thing. He'd be all over it. What he was all over was some unofficial lost time, which meant another stop at the 6-9. All the better to bill you for, my dear.

Rook went over to Fort Hamilton, calling Big Poppa at Rikers to double-check on Gracey. She was still in ad seg, which meant she was safe.

It would be good to see Blessing again. The real deal, combat Airborne, Intelligence, then CID. They'd worked together to bring down some of the big time Latin Kings. More recently they were bringing down some heavy alcohol while Rook was trying to get one of those Westie holdovers.

Forty-five minutes of bullshit later, Lucas learned that Captain Blessing had retired, which meant that his eye shit he wore that patch for had finally gotten to him. "Wet macular degeneration" he had said last time. You're thinking you get taken out by WMD, it's not going to be that. Another confirmation that life's a bag of crap on a summer day.

Rook got on the FHP at 92nd Street and then the Verrazano. Plenty of time to make his appointment with Phelps. You do not keep Warren G. Phelps Esquire waiting, especially when he's charging you Boardwalk and Park Place per hour.

Back at the St. Claire his answering machine was flashing red and the sofa using some hypnotic charm to get him to lie down. The phone message was from Warren's new secretary most politely indicating that Attorney Phelps will have to adjourn their meeting until later that afternoon, but "he had seen to that issue he called about." Warren Phelps saying he's "seen to that issue" meant Warren had used his magic and his muscle so there was no replay of what happened at Rikers. It also meant for him to stay out of it now.

Rook took half of one of the pills DiBona gave him so that he could get a couple of hours and recharge his batteries. When he woke up, he only felt halfway for shit. There was a message from Catherine Wren calling to say she had two tickets for the opera next week.

He called her. She didn't get the phone until the sixth ring.

"Everything alright?" he asked. Six rings is too many.

"Drying my hair, Lucas it's nice to hear your voice. You sound better."

"Not good enough to go to the opera, Catherine."

"Of course not. Father's tickets. I'm to meet him there, so I thought we could have dinner together."

"Only if it's raw fish."

"Wonderful. This great new sushi place just opened."

"Just kidding. I was thinking more like the Carnegie."

"That could work, Lucas. I'll call you when I know more about Father's schedule. I miss you."

"See you soon, Cat. See you soon," he told her.

Things weren't going too bad considering he just had been shot and his blind friend, Grace, was looking at a homicide prosecution for saving his sorry ass. Maybe another hour of shut-eye, but lying down just made him agitated. Rook got up and tried shadow boxing to get the crazy out of his head. Too bad that he punched like a girl now and even that hurt. You're being busy, maybe you forget you're a pussy, so he went to his office to see what was doing. The answer was nothing, which was no surprise, except that the fancy lady called from Phelps' office that an opening had just appeared on his schedule if he would like to come over now.

Rook met Manny as he was leaving. A surprise since he was supposed to be locked up. He looked bad, and not just with that gray jailhouse color that everybody except the animals or the fags came out with.

"You're wondering what I'm doing here, Rook."

"I'm way past wondering about anything, Emmanuel. You alright?"

"I'm alright being out and I thank you for being good with my kid. Besides that, I got a tumor in my head the size of a golf ball."

"You need me for anything, Manny, let me know." Why does bad things happen to good people, some jerkwad was talking about on the tube the other day. Because life blows, that's why.

16

You're going to Phelps' office, you don't dress like a street person, but the jogging suit was going to have to do, because with not working out and still wearing the vest, his tuxedo just wasn't going to fit. About that he's walking around with Kevlar, which by now even he knew was nuts, maybe he should talk to Cholly the shrink about it. Then again, maybe he shouldn't.

Warren had moved his office right after he had finessed the situation in Philly. The U.S. attorney had to be "dissuaded," a Warren Phelps word, that Rook's taking out a baby killer was something that should be going to trial.

Now you're talking Park Avenue with somebody outside polishing brass. Warren had his own suite on one of the floors occupied by Childress, Putnam, and Kroner. In through the mahogany doors, across the thick burgundy carpet, and on to the receptionist with the fancy accent. You're talking with that accent, it's supposed to mean you've got class. It's more like what Cecil Maidman used to say as he took out his cigarette case: "Dress British. Think Yiddish."

How about talk British, be a frigid twat? Miss British Frigid Twat directed Lucas to take a seat, and after Rook's adventure through *National Geographic*, which lamentably was without native chicks showing their titties, she announced that Mr. Phelps would see him. Still the high-backed client's chairs and the big desk, but now a nautical theme, including a massive brass ship's clock in the breakfront behind his desk.

"I didn't know you were a sailor," Lucas said.

"My image consultant got together with my interior decorator. In fact, I think that happens quite often. Those two sensitive fellows thought this makes a statement." The lawyer took a fresh legal pad out of his desk and produced a Mont Blanc the size of a flashlight.

"You're charging me for waiting outside with Ms. Moneypenny?"

Phelps wrote himself a note. "Certainly not," he said. "You know I'm representing your friend, Ms. Savoy. Awful thing about her getting roughed up at Rikers, but I've seen that it shall not happen again. Not only is the Department of Corrections on notice as to possible liability for an action for damages, but I believe that incident is going to resonate with the DA's office and give us some traction. I must reiterate that this consultation is pursuant to my representation of your friend."

"Which mumbo jumbo means you and I have no attorney-client relationship here."

"Sorry about that. I sometimes forget not to be a jackass, but you're right." Warren pushed his chair back.

"I am interested in your assisting me with the owners of record or otherwise of my building, who I believe want to resolve any potential tort actions for my injuries. How's that legal jargon?" Rook said.

"Give me twenty dollars, Lucas, and I'm retained for the purpose of this conversation," the lawyer answered.

Lucas handed him two tens.

Phelps produced a humidor from the credenza behind his desk and offered Rook a Cohiba. "Now that we're done with bullshitting, I could also use your assistance in a certain part of my defense of Ms. Savoy."

Lucas took a cigar to give to Sam.

"What can I help you with, Counselor?"

"I want to know what you think about Grace, about what happened on the roof of your building, and everything about Dwight Graves."

The phone rang. Phelps told Princess Grace to hold his calls and picked up his pen.

"Grace Savoy is my neighbor. My friend too, I guess you could say," Lucas said. "She's blind since she was a kid. Went to the Wade Institute. 'The blind leading the blind,' she always says. I guess it's their motto. Her former lawyer went to school with her. She is a fancy model, vodka ads and so on. I did some security work for her."

"Any history of mental illness?"

"She told me she's been in and out of programs and treatment her whole life. Apparently her parents thought it was easier to have a crazy daughter than one that is pissed she can't see."

"Do you believe she'll be able to help in her defense?"

"She's nuts, but smart as they come."

Warren made some notes. "What else can you tell me?"

"I don't know of any prior issues with the law. She told me her uncle was killed by lightning and that she can hear a pigeon fart a mile away. She's out on the patio a lot, taking care of her flowers, coming over to my place. My .357 was secured in my apartment."

"Do you have any idea why she'd go for it?"

"Somebody had tried to kill her last year, threw this real estate lady off the roof who he thought was Grace and Gracey's dog with her. That was a while ago. Nothing to do with this. She heard somebody on the patio. She got my gun. Dwight Graves shot me, she shot him."

Warren Phelps poured himself a glass of water.

"What was it about Detective Graves and you?"

"He was a dirty cop. I found out about it."

The lawyer waited for Lucas to go on. He didn't.

"What can you tell me about Ms. Savoy shooting him?"

"I'm down. I can't move, but I can see and hear. Dwight's trying to talk her down. She got the magnum, while he's making a play for my Glock. She followed his voice, put three glasers into him."

"Glasers?"

"They call them safety rounds, because they only expand on hitting flesh. Go in like they do and inside it's like a hand-grenade going off. One, two, three, the prick is dead."

Phelps ripped off the pages and put them on the right side of the desk.

"Tell me about your real estate issue," he said.

"The building's going condo, co-op, whatever, which means either I get lucky or I'm moving to Copland, New Jersey. After I get shot, they want to talk to me."

"Any prior security issues in the building?"

"Other than the real estate lady and the dog going airborne off the roof?"

"Not that that is not sufficient for our purposes, yes."

"Just that, for which they put them off-duties into the lobby."

"To give you the false sense of security, and then another detective who is not on official business or in their employ gets free access to the building."

"Here it goes," said Rook. "The rabbit's going into the hat."

"Lucas, I think the district attorney's office has their proverbial head up their ass if they are looking at my client for murder. I also think that I need to do some homework on your real estate matter. In the meantime, I don't think you have to worry about moving to New Jersey so fast."

The intercom rang. "That will be Ms. Churchill reminding me my next appointment is here."

"I like the British touch," said Lucas.

"Bizarre thing's she's an orthodox Jew. Whatever you get on Dwight Graves is going to help Grace, his being 'a dirty cop,' as you say. I do not, however, want the information coming from you. The report will be discoverable by the DA and your association will taint it."

"We're good here then, Counselor?"

"I think we are, Lucas Rook. Enjoy your day."

Rook bid Ms. Churchill a fine *shalom* and a *l'chaim* thrown in and walked a couple of blocks before going crosstown. See what Muskrat had on his super sale, maybe some decent pants for six bucks. The leather jacket he had gotten last time was widely accepted as haute couture.

Lieutenant Jaluski pulled up to him.

"You all done your meeting, Mr. Rook?"

"Couple of beers with some of the bosses from Downtown, Jaluski. Asking me if I know any double-dealing, two-faced cheese eaters looking to give a hand job."

"I got my eye on you, Rook, like I did your brother."

Lucas walked over to the car. "Anytime, anyplace, fuckface."

"Give my regards to your girlfriend, the cop killer," said Jaluski and he pulled away.

Telling a rat squad fuck to go fuck himself would give anybody an appetite. Muskrat would have to wait. And the heart docs would have to turn their heads. There was a decent deli down the block.

Lucas got a seat in the window. Good to watch the world go by without a bother about who was doing what to whoever. And maybe in a hundred years or so he could feel that way for five minutes. Jaluski did come around the block again and some schmuck did get his pocket picked, but neither was enough to distract from the salami and eggs, well-done, rye toast, two cups of coffee, and a piece of coconut custard pie in honor of Dwight Graves, the lying motherfucker, whose life was going to get the kind of eyeball Mother Teresa couldn't stand.

Lucas Rook went back to his apartment. With all the fancy sleight of hand work Phelps could do, maybe he'd own his place before it was all over. New Yorkers talked about their apartment buildings like they owned them. "My building" and so forth.

He was opening a nice cold one when he reminded himself, You're not a total jitbag, you got to remember where Tuze was lying down.

Rook picked up the Merc at Sid's and drove out to the Policeman's Home. Ray Tuzio, who had taught him about the streets and cop life, wearing his Aviators on the job and off, looking like Dean Martin even when he was bringing hell to what was bad out there, was still in the Alzheimer's ward. Everything smelled like crap. One of the three beds in his room was empty. The cop in the other bed had shit himself. Used to be cops, now lost boys with loads in their pants asking for someone to change them.

"Let's go down the hall," Lucas said.

Tuze said something about "knocking on doors" or maybe just "knocking" or "Buy me a knockwurst" or whatever the fuck.

"It's our beat," Rook told him.

A pretend nurse was coming in from catching a smoke. "The officer in Room 106 needs to be cleaned up," said Rook.

"I'll get an aide," the nurse answered.

"I'm sure you will." Rook produced a fifty. "There's an empty bed in my partner's room."

"Yes, Mr. Black was coming out as I was coming in."

Quaint the undertaker shows up to cart one out, he's Mr. Black. "I want Mr. Tuzio to have that open bed next to the window."

Lucas shook the nurse's hand and passed on the Grant. "I come regular, you know," Rook said. "I'll be shaking hands with you nice, he gets that bed."

"I'm sure that can be arranged," she said.

"And maintained."

"Why certainly, unless he had a health issue that calls for him to move to our infirmary."

"I expect the bed will be waiting for him when we come back. I want him to have that window until Mr. Black shows up for him." Rook gave her his tough cop look to seal the deal. Then he walked Ray Tuzio around and brought him back to lie down to sleep next to that window.

Sid Rosen was in the back when Lucas brought the Mercury back.

"That you?" the garageman called.

"Anybody could say 'yes,' Sidney. You got to be careful."

"It's a bad guy, I empty both barrels then call you, Lucas boy."

"I'll drink to that," said Rook.

"I'll drink to John Cameron Swayze after twelve hours in toxic chemicals." He wiped his hands and poured them each a shot. "Ray Tuzio okay?"

Rook downed his Wild Turkey. "Nope," he said, and he tapped his glass for another.

17

Lucas Rook made himself a cup of coffee to start his bowels and the day. He took his .45 into the bathroom to shit and shave, and now he had the doc's clearance to take a decent shower. Things were fucked up, but looking up, which was the best you could hope for if you lived in the real world. More often, it's fucked up. Fucked over. Fucked the fuck up.

Rook got out and patted the wound spots first, then the surgical sites. There was a knock on the door. A man's hand.

"We don't want any," Lucas said.

"District attorney's office. Open up."

Had to be for the grand jury. You got six days to run that after the arrest and only two left, which meant he was going to get their subpoena, talk to Phelps again, and get amnesia.

"You want to slip it under the door is good," he told them.

"Stop busting my balls, Rook. You know I got a job to do. Let me hand you the summons and then go about my business."

"Then let me put some clothes on," which meant just shorts and sweat pants, let them see the bullet holes and what not.

Rook opened the door. The DA's guy was in his twenties. Must know somebody. The kid did a double take at the wounds, then started to read the time and place.

Lucas took the papers. "Now you have a real nice day," he said. "I come across any fender benders, I'll send them your way."

He had been on the stand a hundred times. You know what you're going to say before you go in, even if you don't know what they're going to ask, and you stick to it. Saying you don't remember is okay. Being a smart ass is not. In front of the grand jury you got twenty-three fine citizens eating tuna sandwiches and potato chips who are going to hear a one-sided story. You have the Virgin Mary up there, they're going to bring back an indictment. You're the bad guy or the DA's wanting to turn you into one or you're a stupid fuck, you can get hung out bad because you're up there without a lawyer. They throw you a curve, you got to know to tell the judge you got to take a piss and go out into the hall to ask your attorney before you utter a word so you don't get yourself jammed up with a felony charge yourself.

The DA's going to be hard on Grace Savoy that she shot a cop no matter that Dwight was a pus bag scammer. Warren G. Phelps, barrister extraordinaire, is wanting a certain reality for her that's different than the I got shot by Dwight Graves and that's all I can remember. How exactly it's going to play out at the grand jury is why Warren gets a jillion dollars an hour.

Rook walked over to Joe Oren's to get a decent breakfast, then came back to run the tag and pedigree of the Circuit City ninja, who turned out to be Syreeta Muhammad, born Florence Butler. Syreeta had a sheet for shoplifting, receiving stolen property, theft by deception, child neglect, assault on a police officer and two counts of robbery, one old, one new, which meant the dear lady would be carrying some kind of weapon under that Halloween costume of hers.

A little more digging came up with Jeremy Beck with a Park Slope address as the other actor in two of the pinches that Syreeta took. Sounds like a poor little rich boy with jungle fever. Poor little rich boy who's now as likely as not to wind up receiving a whole lot of jungle love in the prison showers.

If there's a choice between Bed Sty where Syreeta lay her nappy, ninja head and Park Slope, you pay your visit to the 78th Precinct, where it's yuppies sipping white wine rather than where every corner produced a dozen Mike Tysons.

The clipboard Lucas carried made access to the Garfield Place brownstone as easy as his pic-eze tools opened up lover boy's apartment. Fancy prints on the walls, high-end furniture, cheeses in the fridge that were not Velveeta. And surprise, all kinds of Circuit City crap, which meant not only did you have to get with the 68th about who was hitting the store in their precinct, but Zernial at the 7-8 needed to be checked in with. You don't run your job in somebody's backyard without their okay, even if it's after you've been in the perp's apartment. You get that before if it's anything but a pissant job you're running.

There were a couple of decent looking bakeries near the station house, but the first one only sold donuts sweetened by fructose, whatever that was, and no animal products whatsoever, which means it's a bagel, not a donut. The next stop was pay dirt and Lucas Rook went to the precinct like a righteous member of the law enforcement community should.

The desk sergeant was an ugly woman with a peanut growth on her cheek.

"Sign in," she said. "And two forms of ID, please."

Rook told her he was a gold shield off the job and that he was there to see Captain Zernial. This moved her not at all.

"Sign in and two forms of ID."

Rook was on his way out so she could fuck herself and he'd call it in what he had to say when Argentiri came down the steps.

"We got a celebrity in the house," said Billy A.

"A celebrity who's got to sign in and show two forms of ID," said the desk.

"I got this, Martha," said Argentiri.

"It's Sergeant, Detective. And it's still sign in and two forms of ID."

"Right, Martha," Billy told her as he took Lucas off to the side.

"Here to see the boss," Lucas said.

"The cap's on vacay. Chasing them swordfish or whatever. Business or pleasure?" asked Billy.

"I'm doing some work for Circuit City, a return caper. Salt and pepper team, with the salt being yours, a nice little Jewish boy on Garfield who's returning the swag to the store over in the 68th."

"We don't even have the job up. You been to the 6-8?"

Rook put the bag of donuts down and took out one of his business cards. "You're the first to know."

"Appreciate it, Rook. You're a fine citizen."

Lucas wrote down Beck's particulars and the info from Circuit City on the back of one of his cards and handed it to Billy. Cheesy, but it beats flyers or whatnot.

"Nice card. The chess piece and all," said Argentiri. "You want me to let the sector car know you'll be around?"

Rook handed him the bag of donuts. "I'm good, William," he said. Then he went out to his car and rolled to the 68th to give them the other piece.

Mike Piechowski wasn't in the house, which meant a sit-down with Lieutenant Quam, who turned out to be good police despite the fact that he got his rank because he used chopsticks or whatever.

"I'll see whoever's catching rattles Ms. Syreeta Butler's cage," said the lieutenant. "And let the boss know this came from you when he gets back."

"Appreciate it," said Rook. "Billy Argentiri at the 7-8 got the other piece."

Lucas called Raja Searles to give him a heads up on the way back into Manhattan.

"Very good, very good," said Searles. "Should I call the police or will they call me?"

"Give them a couple of days, Raja. They're on it. Call me when you hear from them, or if you don't by the end of the week. They know to ask for you."

"Excellent. What do I do in the meantime? If the crooks come back."

Lucas cut hard to the right to avoid a drifting delivery truck.

"Write down the particulars, then call me. I'll be right out."

"It will be good to get this over with," said Searle.

Not as long as the meter's running, son. Speaking of which, time to do some serious paperwork since New York's finest was going to finish the job for him.

Lucas started his report by thinking about it over a cold beer. His cell rang. Ms. Churchill's British accent announcing that Mr. Phelps was returning his call and ignoring Rook's request that she join him for a vodka martini, shaken not stirred.

"I got my invitation, Counselor," Rook said, "for Gracey's grand jury."

"Of course. We should have dinner. Eight-thirty? I'll have my car pick you up."

"Of course," said Lucas. "I'll wear something clean."

Rook tried to get the report for Circuit City going again, but he was drifting. He needed to lie down less and less during the day, but if he was not going to feel like shit later, maybe fall into his shrimp cocktail, it was nappy time. He unplugged the phone, turned off his cell and stretched out in front of the boob-tube.

A knock on the door. Lucas sat up and reached for his Glock. Another knock. "Lucas. It's Catherine."

He looked at his clock. Two hours had passed.

"I'll be right there," he told her.

Lucas put his .45 on the mantelpiece and let her in. She looked elegant, but drained.

"I was worried about you," she said. "I tried calling you here, but…"

Rook put his arms around her. He had lost muscle and maybe he shouldn't be pressing her as hard to his chest as he used to, but she needed it.

He went into the bathroom for some mouthwash.

"I'm worried about you. I miss you," she called to him.

"I'm up and at it, Catherine. Back to work and what not," he said as he came back into the room.

She was straightening the pillows on his sofa. "Nothing dangerous or anything?"

"I'm good, Cat." He looked at his watch. "You want a fried egg sandwich? And I got some red wine left over from somebody or other's something. I'm supposed to be drinking red wine."

"Perfect," she said. "It will be nice to stay in. Just us two." She tried a smile. "Unless there's another one of those 'jobs' we can do like in New Jersey."

"I've got to meet with Gracey's lawyer tonight, Cat. He just called, until about 10:00, a couple of hours at the most. The only time he's got. I got to leave around eight."

"I believe you, Lucas. The eggs will be just fine. Maybe we'll go out for coffee when you get back."

Lucas went over to the little kitchenette and took out his enamel pan. A hunk of butter, the eggs. One was a double yolker. That used to mean nothing when Kirk was alive and after he got blown away, he used to stare at the frying pan or throw them out. Now they were just eggs, which was maybe good or not.

Rook could hear the tub running in the bathroom.

"You taking a bath, Cat? I'll keep this warm." He put a plate over the frying pan.

"When was the last time you cleaned in here?" she called.

He could smell the bleach or whatever as he walked over to the bathroom. "Halloween. I do the bathroom every Halloween or maybe Thanksgiving. Besides, you're all dressed up."

"Kind of," she said. Catherine had taken off her skirt and sweater.

"And here I am," she said. "Cleaning your bathroom in my bra and panties."

"Yes you are," he said.

The tub was filled.

"The water's fine, they say."

113

"I'm not supposed to soak yet," he told her.

"I understand."

"I don't," he told himself as he moved her back against the sink. He fucked her with his shirt on. And not at all like he loved her, when they were at her place on Sunday afternoon, or even like she was Valerie Moon, who he fucked on his desk, on her kitchen table, once on the hood of his car. He fucked her like he didn't know her, which Catherine Wren could tell, and when she got dressed to eat their egg sandwiches and drink the cheap wine, she felt close to his suffering and far away too. And Lucas Rook felt like he was somewhere else, like up on that roof, or who the hell knew where.

18

Rook wore his funeral suit to his dinner meeting with Warren Phelps. You have the funeral suit and the summer suit. For court you got the sports jacket you got from Muskrat for eight bucks.

The entrance to the Harvard Club on 44th was closed, so Rook went around the corner. Tommy Pannachio was sitting at the welcome desk. They gave each other the what-are-you-doing-here look.

"My disability came through," said Tommy. "About freakin' time." He said *freakin'* quiet enough not to hurt any of the delicate ears that could come by. "Heard you had a dust-up. You okay?"

"Good, Tommy. And I just love this place."

"Me too, Rook. Can't decide whether my youngest should go to Harvard or Staten Island Community College."

A guest walked by with a stick up his ass.

"And with whom shall you be dining, sir?" asked Tommy P.

"I shall be dining with Attorney Warren Phelps, I shall," said Rook.

"Excellent."

"Excellent."

"But please do adjust your jacket, sir. Your heater's showing."

"Of course," said Lucas. "Of course."

Warren was at the table sipping a martini out of a tall glass.

"Tell me again what we're doing here?" asked Lucas as he sat down.

The bow-tie at the next table gave him a tsk-tsk look. He got back a "you don't want me waiting for you outside" look.

"Politics, money. It's always about that, Lucas. Which reminds me, you just wolfed the husband of our state treasurer."

"Tell him his old lady prints me some hundreds, I won't slap him."

The waiter came over. Rook ordered a Yuengling, but settled for a Coors. "You can keep the can," he told the waiter.

"You're a bit wound up," said Phelps.

"You were going to tell me how I become a member of this joint. Some committee or whatever, right?"

"Something like that. Would you like to reschedule, Lucas?" He took a sip of his drink and smiled. "I'll only bill you for one meeting."

"I got other things on my mind, Warren. The court thing for Gracey, I got no concern, the way you do your magic."

"Thank you, Lucas." He sipped his drink. "I do want to talk to you about the claim against your building."

The beer came.

"You should know," said the lawyer, "a civil suit has been filed against Ms. Savoy on behalf of the estate of Dwight Graves, deceased."

Lucas took a deep drink. "Doesn't surprise me a bit. And I'm betting the liar, I mean lawyer's Felix Gavilan."

"Excellent detective work, Detective."

"Swarmy, fag, grave-digging pus bag."

"I insist," said the bow tie.

"Don't," said Rook.

"Shall we adjourn to a private room, Lucas?" asked Phelps. That expensive word again.

"I'll be a good boy, Warren. I'm not happy this friend of mine, my neighbor who's blind's in a jackpot because I can't see it coming."

"I understand," said Phelps. "But this evening let us focus on any claim or claims you may have."

"I think I'm going to take a raincheck, Counselor. Send Mister Madame Treasurer or whatever the fuck behind me a drinky poo with my compliments."

"I'll do that," said Phelps. "However, let us do try and continue."

"I'll go easy on the surly," said Lucas.

"Of course," said Phelps as he picked up the menu.

The food was only okay, but the alcohol was what it should be. Rook told Phelps what he wanted to know, then left before coffee and cigars so that none of the cozy members got smacked.

He walked a couple of blocks before he got a cab down to his office. Nothing much to do there except the heavy bag in the basement, which if he went after like he wanted to, the incisions and the holes in him would need Doc DiBona again.

Used to be the only tenant who would be at 166 after hours would be the freak photographer who did the bird noises, but he was now wherever freaky photographers who put plastic bags over their heads go to do their bird noises forever. Now, with the new front to the building and the other upgrades, there were a half dozen business working late, like the architect business that moved in and what not. Which meant there would be smokers outside the building and people on the elevator. They said "good evening," they were about to get cracked.

Nobody got in his face, which meant a straight run up to his relocated office without the waiting room and therefore without the rate bump. The answering machine was blinking. Owls Miksis had another domestic case if he wanted. This time one butch lesbian wanting to track down the other carpet muncher who ran off with their kid who was really neither of theirs, but some podiatrist's who had using his refined skill of jacking off to pay his way through school. No thank you, dueling Lesbos. No thank you, Owlsie.

The night is fucked, sitting with all these assholes and acting like he's half one of them himself talking about filing a lawsuit himself. The old days, you would get shit faced, go see one of Heddy's girls on the Upper East Side, then down to Mott Street to eat yourself into a MSG stupor. Drive around until it was time to start your shift at a 24-hour ham and eggs joint and three cups of coffee.

Now he goes back to see Catherine like he's supposed to, there's going to be a fight. Better he get shit faced. Maybe call Valerie, but that was bullshit now, too. Even she couldn't put up with him tonight. It was all fucked. So was the grand jury. And Kirk? What the fuck Graves is saying that his little brother by less than a couple of minutes was dirty. What the fuck was that about?

Out came the bottle of Jamison's he kept for paying clients or for Valerie if she wanted. Or for tender moments like this that he was feeling like the world was one big turd.

Maybe he should go check on Ray Tuzio at the Policeman's Home again. Cross them up that he was out again so soon. Maybe even Tuze would be half awake. Rook called Owls Miksis to tell him no about the dyke job, maybe shoot the shit, but he got Owls' machine. The potty down the hall beckoned. The phone was ringing when he got back. Wrong number. Lucas poured himself a drink. A bad thing. You're drinking alone and feeling life's the cat's box on a summer's day it is, you're halfway to swallowing your gun.

Rook got up and got out into the New York night. He grabbed a cab back to Sid's and tinned the immigrant fuck taxi driver out of the fare even though the immigrant fuck hadn't done a thing, and the shield was for shit since he retired off the job.

Rosen was not in, but Lucas let himself in. Things were getting way fucked. He called Valerie on her cell. She was waitressing her fine ass off and would be done at two if he could wait that long. Rook sat at Sidney's desk and poured a Wild Turkey. Then another. Something to be proud of when you can mix your alcohol and not puke on your shoes. He'd walk the dog to keep it fair, but Sidney must have taken the pooch with him. There's a way to avoid a raft of life's putrid mess. You get a dog. You call it Bear. Bear croaks, you call the next one Bear. Maybe you call some half- assed stranger like he's your brother Kirk, then Kirk's not dead in the street anymore either.

Rook went over to Joe Oren's and let himself in the back. Call hello so you don't catch a shotgun saying hello first, or so you're not catching Joe nailing the manicurist girlfriend which he has to do there because it's not right with Jeanie still at home and the girlfriend's married. Nobody's home. Ham and eggs. Too many eggs. Fuck it. Coffee. Nothing.

Lucas looked at his Glock .45 on the counter. Not good. Not good. He picked up the phone in the back. Got to be the post traumatic stress shit. He dialed Cholly Hepburn's number then hung up.

He called Catherine to say he was on the way back to his place, but that he was a little fucked up. She asked if she should wait. "A lot fucked up," he told her. She said she understood. "I appreciate it, Cat," he said. "I'll be better in the morning." He went back to his apartment. The new West Indian or East African with the mandatory smile was asleep at the front desk. Probably from working three jobs so he could send money back home to his family so they could get Direct TV in their mud hut.

It was dark upstairs. He shut down the alarm and his own back-up, then checked the spot that had replaced where Gracey had found his .357 to put down Dwight. The new Glock was there. The reflection from the open bathroom door gave him enough light to see that there weren't visitors.

Lucas turned on the TV to warm up the place and took two cans of Yuengling out onto the patio. The lights in the office building across the way were on. The hawk that ruled this part of the New York sky had flown away. Fatter pigeons elsewhere. New York was filled with them. And fat fuck diabolical fat men, oily fat politicians. Felix Gavilan, the Cuban-born Atlanta lawyer, was a fat fuck diabolical oily fag lawyer, who whether he liked it or not was going to be getting fucked in his ass by somebody who wasn't going to be kissing him afterwards.

Even through the first cold beer whose alcohol content joined all that had come before on this glorious night, Rook remembered Gavilan's cell phone number, which he had seen enough on the calendars, business cards, refrigerator magnets.

Gavilan picked up on the fifth ring.

"Guess you didn't want to be talking with your mouth full," Lucas told him. "Tell little Pedro I didn't mean to interrupt."

"I don't like that kind of talk," said Gavilan, who was a fag, but not a punk.

"Then you won't like this either, Fidel. You go after my friend, Grace. I see you, and I will, I'm going to hurt you permanently."

"You are being quite a rude fellow, Lucas. And besides that, you don't understand what's going on."

"I understand you won't see it coming and you're not going to like it. Now you give Ricky or whoever a big kiss and tell him to hold you tight. Because if I come after you, you know what that means."

Lucas hung up and popped the second Yuengling. He felt better. Maybe he should write that all down and send it off to Oprah, a new technique or whatever, you call somebody up in the middle of the night, threaten to beat them to death, then you sleep like a baby.

19

Lucas Rook sat around the courthouse half the day waiting to be called for his testimony before the grand jury on whether or not Grace Savoy blew away Dwight Graves, which she did, and whether that was Murder One, which it wasn't, except in the mind of the chief of the DA's unit, who was a career-hungry loser.

Another hour and a half went by, which Lucas passed by taking a leak a couple of times and engaging his musical talents of making popping sounds with the Snapple lids, both irresistible results of two ice teas. Then a newbie came in to tell him that he would not be called today, but that he remained on call and that he should not discuss the case with anybody, which Lucas remarked what case and that the three-piece suit must make his mother really proud, but it was a dead giveaway that he had probably just passed the bar exam.

Why the case hadn't been called could be for lots of reasons. Least likely was that their calendar got screwed up that it had to be pushed past the six-day mandatory. Anyways, now would be a good time to start to get some muscle back so he could deliver what his meanness was calling for, which right now was a bad beating to Felix Gavilan, Esquire. Reminder that Felix's personal secretary, though no doubt a bone smuggler of the highest order, looked like he could handle himself and that chromed-up automatic he carried.

Lucas Rook went back to the St. Claire and put on his sweats and a pair of steel tips and the Kevlar with the titanium heart piece, which he now knew was shithouse mouse crazy to be wearing. But he wasn't ready yet for the diver's vest, even with only some of the weights.

He fast walked over to Hudson Street, not running yet which was half-assed, but that's all there was right now. And how do you get back the muscle mass without tearing an ab or an intercostal or your pec, when you've taken three slugs and been cut open. Impressive though that he now knew what some of the muscles were, even though he couldn't work them.

He felt like shit when he got back, which the drinking last night was most likely the cause of, plus he hadn't done anything worth anything since he got shot. Lucas drank some tap water with lemon, then started up a couple of grilled cheeses which was interrupted by his throwing up into the kitchen sink. Not a particularly appetizing addition to his culinary efforts, but at least there weren't those black coffee grounds coming up which meant he was bleeding internally. Just the fact that he was out of shape and couldn't do anything with that good old feeling that he needed to rip somebody's head off.

Rook chewed a couple of Pepto tabs, reminding himself that would make his shit turn black after it calmed his stomach down. He stretched out on the sofa. Fuck it. He got up and ate some saltines, a drunk man's best friend, opened a brew and ran the tub.

The warm bath was good and he started to drift off, which wasn't good. You could drown in the tub. He had seen it more than once on the job. He got up and turned the shower on cool and then got out of his apartment, which obviously was no good to be in now. The billing and report on the Circuit City thing would have to wait. Time to get rolling on Gracey's situation.

You got a case to run, you run it. Plenty of shitbirds around. Fat ones, skinny ones. Old ones, new ones. Maybe you get lucky fast and come up with something that blows up the case against Gracey. Unlikely, but worth the thought. Like you fall asleep loaded and it wakes you up, Jessica Simpson licking your balls.

Too bad that Hy Gromek was dead. One way or the other he'd have something that could be used to dirty up Dwight to help Gracey. Hy was a good guy, even if he was on the pad, which no way he wasn't, he's partnered up with Dwight Graves. But taking a little numbers cash here and there's not the same as what DG was running to keep himself in six-hundred-dollar suits and hundred-dollar ties.

Shanty McCloskey was Dwight Graves' partner before Hy was. "Shanty" not because he was Irish, but because he married a girl whose father was a big builder out on Long Island when it was getting all built up. Shanty would've been a millionaire a hundred times over if he had stayed married, but that couldn't happen because he was a bad drunk and an incurable cunt hound. Instead he winds up living in a run-down claptrap on the back of somebody's lot.

But Shanty was smart and tough enough to put in his thirty, the last eighteen living with somebody who could put up with his nonsense and being a cop's old lady. Last heard, Mr. and Mrs. Shanty McCloskey owned a Dairy Queen in North Bergen. Take a run out to Bergen and get a hot fudge sundae from McCloskey, and maybe something on the dead black bastard lying fuck Dwight Graves. The only thing that would have made it perfect would be you could somehow bill it to Raja Searles and the return scam.

Lucas went over to Rosen's garage. Good time to take the Avanti out. Kirk had been the motorhead and this had been his favorite, the '63 black fiberglass coupe with the mufflers that sounded like Vaughn Monroe. Which maybe he wasn't going to have to sell so he didn't have to move to Jersey if Phelps got anywhere in getting the building to pay up.

Rosen was walking some yuppy fuck to the door and patting her on the back.

"I'm sorry, I just can't help you, dear. I just don't work on Mini Coopers. I'm sure your baby will be just fine until the dealer can get you in."

"Going to take the Avanti, Sidney."

"She's running a little hot, Lucas, like my old lady didn't used to."

"Just making a run over to North Bergen."

"The home of James J. Braddock. The Bulldog of Bergen. The 'J' stood for Walter." The garageman got up to get some keys off the board and underhand a set to Rook so they could make a hole to get the coupe out.

"I did not know that," said Lucas.

"After he beat Baer, they backed him out of a fight with Schmeling so there wouldn't be a Nazi champion. Joe Gould gets Braddock ten percent of all Joe Louis makes so he gets the shot," said Rosen. He swung a Volvo out and onto the sidewalk. Rook followed with a Buick that smelled of stale Marlboros.

"You want I should ride out with you, Lucas boy?"

"I'm good, Sidney. Just going out to see an old friend and get me some Dairy Queen."

"You do, bring me back a couple of bags of those bars, chocolate for me, butterscotch for Bear. Chocolate's poison to dogs."

Rook started up the coupe. "I do know that, Sidney. And I owe you one of your books or two." Kind of a bitchy thing to say if Sid doesn't ask. Well, another pleasant side of being shot or the meds or whatever.

Lucas took the Lincoln Tunnel then I-95 into Jersey. The Avanti wasn't running hot and the new brake kit Rosen had put in was doing what it was supposed to even when the douche bag in the Mercedes up ahead stopped short.

The McCloskey's ice cream store was on Kennedy Boulevard. America at its craziest, Kennedy. If you believe the lone gunman, single bullet theory, then you believe in Santa. You're the President and your baby brother's the AG, no way both of you can turn out dead. A decent story he heard is they got it for killing Marilyn Monroe, poison suppositories up her ass from the Feds, like that. So you kill Joe D's wife, this is what you get. And the fat, drunk brother, who should get it for leaving Mary Jo what's-her-name to drown, he's like some liberal icon instead of the turd he really is with roads named after the douchebag family.

Shanty was in the store, but he wasn't going to have much to add to what was going on, being he was strapped in a wheelchair with a bib to catch his drool. Two kids with bad skin were working in the place.

"Can I help you?" asked one.

Shanty made some noise.

"It's alright, Pop," said pockmarks.

"How you doing, Shanty?" said Rook. "Nice place you got here."

McCloskey made some other noise.

"Hot fudge sundae, wet walnuts," said Rook. He went over and got the bars from the freezer.

McCloskey shook his head like don't charge this guy or something, but it was lost in the translation. Lucas paid full boat and went out to the parking lot to make magic with the red plastic spoon.

Two Spanish dudes pulled up in an unmarked van. Lots of Spanish, particularly from South America, in Bergen and Hudson County now. Sacco, who was the mayor, must be a saint. And a magician too, particularly because the Public Safety was run by some lady. Maybe she kept the peace by baking cookies.

Vans are the vehicle of choice of lots of bad guys, particularly serial killers, rapists and the like. If you're boosting, you roll in, load up the merch, roll on out. Pancho gets out and goes into the Dairy Queen. A couple of seconds later, the other Pancho swings around the back.

Rook puts his sundae on the seat and brings his Glock .45 to deal with the two pus bags about to hit Shanty's ice cream joint. He comes in the front door so as not to spook anybody. Pus bag numero uno is around the counter, a black revolver at his side. The second one's playing lookout. The pimply kids are in the corner with Shanty, whose eyes are as big as his Brownie Bomba-rino Banana Split.

Pablo's into the cash register when he feels Rook's automatic at the back of his head.

"Say hello to my little frien'. I got that right?" said Rook. "Now drop your pistola. Hands up slowly."

The greaser does. Rook puts the piece of shit .22 in the freezer.

"Your running buddy's out back. Call in Pancho. We have a little what's-his-name, *problema*. But no harm, no foul."

Frito Bandido calls in Pancho number two. Rook jacks him. The shit heel drops like a rock.

"Don't forget the dessert," Lucas tells the first Pancho as he presses his .45 to the guy's eye. Then the fucker's hands go into the hot fudge dipping thing. Pancho screams, the pimply boys cheer. McCloskey makes a bunch of sounds. Rook tells the ban-dido, "This is my *hermano's* spot, *compadre. Comprende?*"

Rook drove back into the city. He hurt from all the work. Shanty McCloskey *was* a helluva cop. So *was* Ray Tuzio, and McCul-lagh. This *was* brother Kirk's car.

Too much *was*. Christ, he *was* a gold shield instead of writing up his bills and halfway cheating on them. He used to be able to run a perp down in any alley instead of walking with a fucking cane at the end of the day and now still feeling like he was halfway shot up.

And what does he have to show for all that stuff that is now *was*? He got Gracey in a world of shit for saving his life. Shysters are trying to throw him out of his apartment and shysters are trying to keep him in it. This ain't the way he saw it: *was*, shit, and shysters.

Lucas thought about calling Catherine Wren, but he was still as mean as last night. He tried Valerie instead, who was put off only by not getting fucked and not drinking cold beer. The number was disconnected. He tried it again and got her answering machine.

Things were not going good. They hadn't been. Even tuning up the two greaser bad guys didn't seem to matter. Not good. Fucked-up.

Rook called Cholly the Shrink, who said he'd call him back in an hour. A colleague was coming in who had decided that it wasn't necessarily appropriate that he was getting blowjobs from his niece.

20

Rook opted for a consult with Dr. Jack Daniels instead of following up with Cholly Hepburn. There was a new joint around the corner, a chi-chi place that catered to a clientele that thought Cosmopolitans weren't for assholes.

The bartender had been around enough to suggest that Lucas find a place "that did not specialize in anything that Liza Minnelli might be having." That and a double Jack and water which cost twelve bucks convinced Lucas to move on.

His recent adventure in the Dairy Queen reminded him that while he might be feeling like he was falling apart, he was not dead yet, which called for a celebration that he wasn't no *was*.

He flagged down the first cab not driven by somebody who should be buried upside down in a spider hole and directed him to the nearest hot dog stand.

"You know a driver named Haak, a fiend for grape soda?" Rook asked.

"As of a matter of fact, I do. I'm his cousin by marriage. Bobby passed away, I'm sorry to say. One, two, three, he's sick, he's dead."

Lucas paid the meter and got out. He walked a couple of blocks and found himself another stand. Two dogs, loaded, and a grape soda in memoriam.

The Sabrette's and the condiments neutralized some of the residual ugly in him, so that when Rook got to Miata's, he was alright. A good thing. You go into a cop bar being an asshole, something unpleasant's going to happen.

The place was jammed.

"Somebody's racket?" Lucas asked.

"Look what the cat dragged in," called Johnny Morris, who was down the bar with Fain. Christ, they were all there. Nucie, Dunlop, Mesirov, Antopol, Welby.

"How you holdin' up?" said Nucie.

"He's good. He's good," said somebody in the crowd.

"Better than Mr. Bojangles, who got what he got coming," said Andi, coming over with a beer in each hand. "We're drinking to Obie, Dobie, whichever," she said.

One of the twins was behind the bar, wearing his dirty derby and slinging drinks. The other came out of the gents and joined him.

"You ain't never seen these two jokers together," said Johnny. "You just don't."

"I figured there was only one of them boys to begin with," said Fain.

"To the happy couple," called somebody, raising up his glass.

"Them two?" asked Dunlop. "I don't think so."

"Obie's getting hitched," said Nucie.

"It's my brother," Obie said.

"He's fucking with you," Dobie said.

"Let's drink to that," said a big man who could have been Bill Klein, but wasn't.

"*Fidelis ad mortem*," called somebody. The cops' toast, "Faithful until Death." The cops' motto, but what that dead fuck Dwight Graves said when he was drinking to Kirk and lying his dead black ass off. Lucas lifted his glass, but did not drink.

"The banquet's in the back," said Obie. "Eat up, drink up. My brother's paying for it."

"He is," said the other bartender in the derby.

"Well, I'm not," said Nucie as he went back to the cold cuts.

Lucas went for some potato salad and whatever. Subs D'Lesandro was sitting in a booth with two other cops. The colored guy he had seen before. The other one looked like some college type. Subs tried to get out, but the college kid was too busy talking about nothing to notice.

"Yo," said D'Lesandro, "you want me to whip it out right here, I'm taking a leak in about two seconds either way, kid."

College slid out of the booth, which was not easy the way everybody was moving back to the eats. D'Lesandro caught up to Rook.

"You alright?" Subs asked him.

"Me, I'm good. How you doin'?" asked Lucas.

"Going to get some of this spread." The line moved slowly. Fast Eddie was up at the front touching everything with his bare hands.

"That's what we got forks for," Andi said, who was right behind him.

They moved towards the promised land of ham, cheese, and salami. The white mounds of macaroni and potato salad and cole slaw were dwindling. Lucas filled his plate.

"You hear from Banko?" he asked Subs.

"Florida. I think. He got himself a condo down there. Near Tampa or something."

"You?" asked Lucas to cover he was asking, not making small talk.

"Me?" said Subs. "I'm staying here. Two more, I got my thirty in, I move to Maryland to be near my daughter and her husband, my grandkids." D'Lesandro made himself a ham and cheese.

Rook went back to the bar. Morris and the big guy who could have been Bill Klein were going at it pretty good. You got some guys liquored up and they got iron on them's not a good idea even if they are cops. The big guy pushed Morris, which gets him popped pretty good because Johnny used to box. And then there's a lot of pushing and shoving.

"Take it outside, take it outside," Obie-Dobie says.

"I'm not going nowheres," says the big guy and he makes another move at Johnny, who slips him, but does not lay hands.

"We alright?" says the bartender.

"We're good," Morris says. The big guy nods.

"Pour me one for the road, Obie-Dobie," said Lucas. He put a twenty on the bar. "For the happy couple," he said.

Rook went back to his apartment, liquored up and tired, but with the info from D'Lesandro, no way was he going to be able to put his head down even though it was late and he was drunk. A final consultation or two with Doctor Daniels dulled the pains in his chest and the circus in his head. Lucas put his .45 on the end table and fell asleep on the sofa.

There were jumbled-up dreams and the phone ringing which somehow became part of the movie marathon going on in his head. Rook got up and popped himself a Yuengling. Ten-thirty is not a good time to report to the grand jury room at nine. He checked the message machine. An assistant DA named Nussbaum saying that he need not report today, but should report tomorrow, which spared a lot of shit about why he hadn't. How about I got wasted and slept through your monkey party and I did not piss the bed.

He dry-swallowed some Advils, then took a shower. There was a nice bruise from something. Wonderful, at least the aspirins were thinning his blood the way they were supposed to.

Rook went over to Joe Oren's. The breakfast trade was done. Sam in the back doing his clean and prep to get ready for lunch, Joe in the last booth doing some paperwork. A couple in the second booth. Two people at the counter, one of them packing in the small of his back.

Lucas went over to Joe.

"He alright, the balding guy at the counter?"

"Never saw him before. Another reason doing this paperwork's a pain. I'm not watching everything. My accountant says I should get a bookkeeper. I tell him he cooks the books as good as I cook what I cook, maybe I can."

Rook sat down next to the man with the gun. "Nice day, nice place," he said.

"I would say so," said the man.

"Your first time here?"

The guy stirred his tea. "I know you?"

"Lucas Rook, retired off the job."

"So you're probably wondering why I'm sitting at this counter with a firearm on my person." He took a bite of his toast. "I'm having breakfast is all." He sipped his tea. "I'm one of the good guys, just passing through. Had the Western omelet, which was tasty." He got up and smoothed his tie. "Nice place, nice food. Maybe I'll stop in again I'm ever back this way." He paid and left.

Joe came behind the counter and poured Rook a cup of coffee.

"New friend?" he asked Rook.

"Cold fish. Which makes him a fed, or a statie. He's wearing decent clothes," said Joe. "So I make him for a fed."

"Samuel, you back there?" called Rook.

"I am," said the cook. "Breakfast or lunch? The way you're sounding, you're telling Sam it's breakfast, but I'm betting your body's telling you that it needs more than that. You let Sam fix you up some steak and eggs, which is what you need."

"You're right, sir. Steak and eggs it is."

"And grits," said Sam.

"And grits," said Lucas.

Joe Oren poured himself a cup of coffee and sat down at the counter.

"Jeanie found herself a nice boy."

"That's good, Joe."

"A Jewish kid, but alright. Hard working, going to school at night. Jeanie said she wants you to meet him. That his uncle was a cop."

Rook finished his coffee. "Where's he from?"

"From Jersey," he said. "Also when you meet him, the kid's name's David, David Komisar, like the Russian government, like that. When you meet him try not to scare him to death, Jeanie says that I halfway did that."

"With a 'C' or 'K,' his last name?" Lucas asked.

"Appreciate that," said Oren.

Sam brought the steak, eggs and grits out for Rook and sat at the counter for a cup of coffee. The three of them, like everything was alright.

Lucas Rook went back to his apartment, brushed his teeth and after a little bit of spadework, called Joe Oren to tell him that the Jewish kid was okay. Then he got back on his computer to find Banko and then book a little trip to Florida, where he meant to squeeze retired New York City Detective Herbert Banks for whatever he had on Dwight Graves, who he had partnered up with after Hy and before Shanty did. And if Banko looked at him sideways, or opened his mouth about Kirk, he'd beat the daylights out of him.

21

Rook went through the extra paperwork to bring his Glocks, which included a copy of his Pennsylvania carry permit he got the last time down the Turnpike. Florida had reciprocity with a number of states, which would have included New York along with Pennsylvania if Albany didn't have its head up its ass, which it did about a lot of things.

The last time Rook was in Florida was also a quick trip. That one for the sleazebag lawyer to get a document signed by an even bigger sleaze who deserved it coming true he takes a header down to the asphalt. Whether Herb Banks was going to get the ugly treatment this time down was up to him.

Sitting next to Lucas not in first class was a hottie in a business suit, coming back from some kind of pet convention. He didn't get even her business card, which is the worst insult you could get from somebody in sales. So let all that independence shit help her with her sample bag or whatever that was stowed on top.

Things are going good. You're carrying legal, there's a good bump up on the car rental, and travel to Lakeland from the Tampa Airport in less than an hour. Have his conversation with Dwight's old partner, get what he needs, and be back on the six o'clock with no trouble.

Lucas knew nobody there, although if he needed it, Tony had a condo over in Orlando. The research he did before his flight had given him Bank's address. It had also produced Bank's phone number and an aerial photo of his building, which some geek at

Google probably thought was cute, but definitely was only an invitation for bad guys in stocking masks to pay a visit.

You're in town for a couple of hours and you're carrying, you got to know who the locals are. Maybe check in. He got off the computer that Lakeland had some scumbag kill a deputy sheriff and his K-9 partner a while back and took 68 rounds for it. The chief's Roger Boatner and Charles Thompson is under him if you got to drop a name or make a call. You also got it in your head that Bob Evans is a good name if you want a decent cup of coffee and breakfast, which anybody who's been on the job could do 24/7. Lucas popped a Perc with his second cup of coffee and swung over to Viewpoint Court.

The years had not been good to Dolly Banks. She had put on more than a couple of pounds, and that face which had artfully sucked a hundred cocks had dropped. She was wearing glasses and did not recognize him.

"Can I help you?" she asked.

You can suck me dry, like you're famous for, he thought. "Is Banko in? I used to work with him."

Dolly took her glasses off. "Of course, dear," she said. "I'll make coffee. Let me get him on the phone. Herbert's at work. He only works part time up the way for the real estate. Herbert's at work now."

So much for Dolly using her head for anything other than your shorts.

"I'll be back in an hour or so."

"He'll be wanting to get right home when I tell him who's here."

"He's up the street, Dolly, at the real estate? I'll go surprise him."

"You do that, dear," she said. "He'll like that fine."

"I guess a blow job's out of the question," Lucas said. But it didn't register and she smiled as she closed the door.

There were three realtors within the first two blocks. Lucas found Banko at Perr's Real Estate. Herbie wasn't selling condos. He was unclogging toilets since he came out of the back with a tool belt around his waist, which if it doesn't come off, you don't get within his arm's reach.

"Can I help you?" asked the receptionist with a smile that had been lacquered on.

"I'm interested in one of the new properties on Wildflower that are going up. I'm an old friend of Herbert Banks."

"Now who would this be?" said Banko as he came towards the front. "Hell's bells," he said. "Excuse me, Sondra. It's Lucas Rook." He wiped his hand on the rag hanging from his waist.

"Well, how you doin'?" said Herbie. "I'm keeping busy, as you can see. Only three, four hours a day at the most. You know, supplement the pension. I'm right down the street. You looking to move, down here's a nice place. I miss the winter though."

Talking too much. As likely as not to hide his guilt that his old partner had shot Rook as that he got a package that could choke a horse underneath his floorboards.

"You want to come by the house? Dolly'll be glad to see you."

"I stopped by. She told me where to find you."

"Good, good. You can follow me over." Banks unhooked his tool belt and took it with him.

So there's another chance to see the lovely Dolly whose brains seem to have gone the way of her face. But also some time to sniff around. Already something's not kosher, Banko's not clocking out or whatever. Then again, maybe it's just the paranoia which any cop worth a damn has got plenty of, not to mention you've just been shot three times by somebody from the job who tells you your twin brother was a dirty cop which got him dead. So maybe like they say, just because I'm paranoid doesn't mean I'm wrong. And if Graves was dirty, which was what would help Gracey, no way Herbie wouldn't know about it, and dollars to decent donuts, he was a piece of shit himself.

If Banks' house had any more pictures of kittens in it, Herbie and Dolly would have to change their last name to Hallmark. Pictures of kittens everywhere, climbing up a rope, chasing their tails, making little kittie turds. And about a thousand figurines. Probably better for Banko though that she's collecting them now instead of cocks, which she was collecting back then.

Herbie took Lucas into the breakfast room where they entered another realm of *chatzka* heaven. About three dozen snow globes.

"The wife got me started. I got thirty-four now. Reminds me of back up North."

They sat waiting for the coffee until Banko realized that it wasn't coming. "Let me give her a hand," he said. "She forgets things sometimes."

A quick look around the room revealed nothing of interest but the fucking snow globes. Too bad none of them had little kitties in them.

"Dolly's going to lay down," Herb announced when he came back. "She hasn't been feeling well." He sipped his coffee. "Well, let's get to why you're here, Lucas Rook."

"And what's that?"

"You're not here to shake all them snow globes to get them all going at the same time. You want to work me for what I know."

Lucas tried the coffee. It was for shit and decaf. "I'm listening, Banko."

Banks picked his cup up and then put it down again. "Twenty questions, whatever. I'll give you the straight skinny about Dwight. Or maybe about your brother."

"I'm still here."

"They worked a couple of cases together, Kirk and Dwight. Once I was IOD. Another time on vacay. You're asking me what that means? DG was always around the edges, picking up a little extra. You're asking me whether he was on the take for anything serious, not that I know of."

"DG or my brother?"

"Good cop, my partner. Your brother, Kirk, I don't got much to say about. Young. Alright guy from what I know." He finished his decaf. "The pricks who shot him, they deserved what you gave them. And more."

"Etillio, Herbie. Tell me about him."

Banks started one of the snow globes. "You're sounding like IAB."

"That's bullshit, Banko. Look, nobody's trying to squeeze your shoes. My brother's dead, that's that. I'm just looking for anything that can help the blind girl who saved my ass."

"I heard about that. You're asking me about Etillio and Dwight, I know nothing about that. I gave you what I got. Etillio was mobbed up. Him and his crew were bad news. I was a good cop. So was DG. So was your brother. That's all I have for you. Now I got to get back to work. People to see, broken windows to fix."

"Appreciate it, Banko." Rook got up. Banks didn't. "Some collection of them snow globes you got."

"I don't count the doubles. The wife got some twice. Sorry I got nothing else for you."

Lucas stopped at the Bob Evans. He had some shit from Banks he wanted and some he didn't. DG was on the pad. Kirk wasn't clean as the driven snow in those crazy glass things. And Herbie had more he wasn't saying. Finding out how much would mean maybe a trip back to lovely Lakeland, Florida after some research to check on Herbie's real estate transactions. Doing that was probably halfway whacko, but so was living with a million kitties and a half million snow globes.

Rook finished his decent cup of coffee and a piece of cheesecake that only hinted at something from New York. Then he passed Banko's place a couple of times to shake his tree a little bit and drove to the airport.

By the time Rook got back to his apartment he had a pounding headache, which the boob tube and three Advils put to rest. *The Man in the Iron Mask* on Turner. He had Jane Fonda on a bodyguard detail once. "Hanoi Jane" and all that, but still Barbarella. Hot as hell, but crazy as shit, which what do you expect from somebody who's married to Tom Hayden and Ted Turner. *Rebellion in Newark* meets TNT or whatever the fuck.

Lucas started feeling pissed off and restless. He took the elevator down through the kingdom of the rich: dentists, architects, the Martha Raye lady, who got her money because a relative invented the Slinky or something.

He walked the streets until his bad leg started acting up. Like the old days on the beat, trying the doorknobs so the stores were locked up tight. Like the nursery rhyme where all the kids are safe in bed, which was never true anywhere. The night was always filled with whackos who would rape them and kill them in their beds. And that's not bullshit either. That's what the world is.

Rook went up to his room. Maybe he should ride it straight through. Do tomorrow exhausted instead of wired. Maybe not. Maybe Princess Grace was going to call, he should look fresh and charming for tea. He took a Benadryl to fall asleep in his bed like a good little boy, except he was still dressed and his .45 was under his pillow.

The Benadryl didn't do shit. Not being able to fall asleep is one of those fine things about being a cop. You take another pill, maybe you don't wake up at all. So it's back to the sofa and the television. Crazy living like that, but not crazier than it being two o'clock in the morning and you got somebody uninvited coming into your place.

22

"A pair of tits in the night," said Grace Savoy as she came in through the sliders.

"How do I know it's you?" He put his .45 back on the end table.

"I'm the blind one, silly billy," she said.

"Right, and you're supposed to be in jail."

She lay next to him.

"You're naked, Gracey."

"I'm really cold."

Lucas got up and turned on the light.

She took the cigarette from behind her ear. "Light me," she said. "It's so good to be smoking regular again."

Rook found a pack of matches in his dresser drawer. "Would you tell me why you're here? The last time I checked, this was not Rikers."

"Feels like it sometimes."

"Gracey…"

"Okay, Mr. Policeman. I'll spill it. Give it up. Whatever the poor losers still inside call it. But first you've got to brush your teeth."

"You've broke out of jail, in two minutes you're going to be asking if you can lick my balls, but I've got to brush my teeth?"

"Precisely. Morning breath is so *de classe*."

"It's the middle of the night and you're going to tell me what you're doing here."

"I've come over to finally let you fuck me." She sent a stream of menthol smoke away from his voice and flicked the ashes into her hand.

Lucas got off the sofa and went in to take a piss.

"Like a racehorse," she called. "You still got the pressure up."

"Terrific, and you can hear it a mile away."

"You too, by the way you woke up. Or was it my perfume? Heaven Scent by Helena Rubenstein. You can't get it anymore. Even on Canal Street."

"Cut the crap, Gracey," he said as she came into the bathroom. "You're either telling me the truth, which I will be able to verify, or I'm making a call and they'll be a couple of uniforms thrilled to take you back inside. I call in a favor, it'll be two of NYPD's least gentle bull-dykes."

She dropped her cigarette into the toilet.

"I love the sizzling sound that makes. Now if I might freshen up, as you did not supply the lady an ashtray."

Grace washed her hands and then sat down on the toilet. "If you'd like me to hold it until you leave, I can do that."

"No, actually, Grace, listening to a lady escapee taking a piss is one of my most favorite hobbies. Then you can wash your hands again, or lick your fingers or whatever you do, and you're either going to tell me why you're not at Rikers or I'm going to cuff you myself. And don't crack wise about that because I'm not kidding. Meanwhile, you take a piss, I'm pouring myself a beer, for which you'll have something clever to say, but you're not getting one."

Lucas went into the kitchen and popped himself a Yuengling. Grace Savoy did look smoking hot when she came out, doing that fuck me model walk and her lips and nipples glistening from the Lubriderm or whatever she put on them.

"Long or short?" she said.

"What?"

"The story. I know I can get that thing of yours as long as it gets."

"I'm counting to ten, Grace. You won't like me there."

"The long and short of it is they fucked up by not getting the grand jury thing done in time, which means they can't keep me incarcerated. Warren says the DA's office is 'woeful' lately and this is not the first time this has happened. So now we have a preliminary hearing or something like that, at which I don't have to say a thing and I think they can't hang me or give me the electric chair, which would be something to see what would happen to my hair."

"Which doesn't exactly explain why you're telling me coming in off the patio at two o'clock in the morning."

"Right. I need another ciggy. We have a meeting with the lawyers at nine. I hope you'll take me. The paparazzi will be a mess."

"Maybe. But what's this about lawyers? Warren works by himself."

"Things are a little more complicated, Lucas. But they'll be fine since you're coming with me, which is something we should do right now. We can even do hand sex if you want."

"I don't think so, Gracey. And you better not be shitting me."

"I know my way out," Grace said as she left.

Rook checked the clock on his DVR. Terrific. Warren G. Phelps Esquire is sound asleep, dreaming of his monograms or whatever. Maybe Grace was telling the truth and maybe not. He had not been called to testify, so maybe she was. On the other hand, maybe she got transferred to one of those loony-toon facilities where she belonged and she just walked out. Lucas thought of calling Bobby Perez, but let it be. No way did she book from Rikers, which they don't call "The Rock" for nothing.

Lucas cleaned up the place so it would take somebody good from forensics to tell she was there. And now what? Try and get a couple of hours of sleep. Or see what's on the tube. Maybe try a run. Maybe not, unless it's with the second beer in his hand. The channel surfing turns up *The Harder They Fall*. Rod Steiger, Bogart's last movie. Bogie was talking about his journalistic integrity.

Jersey Joe Walcott was giving the Spanish stiff a beating when the phone rang.

"I'm scared, Lucas. Would you come over? I need some cuddling."

"I'm right here, Gracey. And don't worry about tomorrow. Nobody's going to bother you."

"I'm worried about now, Lucas."

"You'll be alright. And I'm right here, but I'm going to be right here alone."

"Okay," she said. "Okie-dokey. I'll smoke and try to relax."

"No dope, Grace Savoy. They're going to piss test you."

"I know. Warren told me."

"Good girl," Lucas said. "I'll see you soon."

"Okay, Prince Charming," she said and she hung up.

Rook heated up a can of soup and watched the movie. The boxing game had always been fixed fights, broken lives. The wise guys doing what they always do and the fighters turning out with their brains scrambled and crapping in their pants.

For him it wasn't bad. He got into the game, then out. First, doing pretty good in the service because he could really bang and had quick feet. Then in the PD. Four pro fights until some gorilla named Herman made him pee blood, which was enough to end the career that was going nowhere anyhow.

Lucas put on his sweats and his steel toes and went out. His old Yanks jacket and a watchman's hat. You don't wear anything PD so nobody takes a sneak at you or asks you to break up a domestic, which can get you hurt bad.

He brought his back-up piece in his outer pocket and went outside into the streets. New York was never black. The office buildings, the cabs. The deliveries. Lucas did the walking thing again, not pushing the heart or the legs, neither of which were ready for what he used to do.

Down to the Bowery, over to the Stroll. Men who should know better getting blowjobs from trannies who said 'thank you, dear' with a James Earl Jones voice. A couple of bums asked him for spare change. One followed along a couple of steps until Rook said he'd kick the life out of him. That made him feel not so much like a punk-ass loser that he was walking instead of going on a run which he did before he got shot.

He kept his pace by Loren's coffee shop, which was just opening up, and then by Sid's garage where Rosen and his dog were comfy-cosy. Rook checked his watch. Five o' clock as Sam came up to open Joe Oren's place.

"You stopping by, I'll be putting coffee on," said Sam.

Lucas held up his hand that he was good and finished his pretend run to his building, whatever that would mean when the lawyers got through. Living there on Gracey's dime if she got through her shit, or on the deal maybe the developers were going to put on the table so he didn't sue the shit out of them, or whatever else Warren G. Phelps could come up with.

A couple of yuppies were coming down the elevator in their running outfits as Rook got on. He gave them his best Sonny Liston look so they wouldn't say anything stupid. "Baleful," that look was described by the sports writers, at least until Liston mailed it in to the fights with Clay and then mysteriously died with a needle somebody else stuck in his arm.

Lucas went upstairs. His tub was running. Either Gracey was at it again or somebody was about to get shot. Grace met him at the door in a pink bathrobe with fluffy slippers.

"I thought you'd like a nice hot bath when you came in, Lucas."

"And you knew when that would be?"

"They called from downstairs. These island primitives think I'm a witch or something, blind, blonde, beautiful."

"Let me cool down, Grace."

"Still worried about your heart?"

"Worried about my balls, Gracey. I don't want them boiled."

"I put lilac in the bathwater. It will make them nice and sweet, but I did it to help you with your injuries. I know all about flowers, Lucas. You know that."

"Right, I remember."

Grace Savoy came close to him. "Let me touch you where you got shot," she said.

"I don't think so, Gracey."

"Then how will I understand?"

"You can take my word for it is how."

"You smell nice, Lucas Rook."

"Terrific. Maybe you'll like my feet when I take these boots off."

"I'm sorry if I'm being a pain in your lovely balls, Lucas." She lit a cigarette. "I'll go home now, but you owe me. Or I owe you. I forget which. Like in the old days, you saved somebody's life they had to take care of you or the other way around."

"I appreciate what happened on the roof, Grace."

"Then you should take me to your breakfast place. Your favorite place, Joe Oren's, before we go to meet the lawyers."

"Okay, I will do that if you get me a cold beer from the fridge and not be telling anybody about me taking a bubble bath."

"So I can't scrub your back, sponge your hoo-hah?"

"I'm good, Gracey. I'll come get you."

Grace was back in fifteen minutes. She looked like an old man.

"For the photographers, so they leave us alone," she said.

"You're probably right, although it would have been easier if I just took you through the boiler room in the basement."

He took a long drink of the beer.

"How did you do that make-up and whatever? Very convincing, Grace."

"Models, especially very successful ones like yours truly, are actors, and any actor worth a damn can do their own make-up and fast change in a jiff. In World War II, Hollywood taught the

145

spies to quick change. You go in the men's room how you are and come out like your grandfather. Besides, I told you my Uncle Bert was a famous drag queen."

Rook got out of the tub. "Right, and he got struck by lightning."

"That's true, neighbor. Can I towel you off?" she asked. "I'll be gentle."

"I don't think so, Gracey. Let me get dressed and we'll go have some ham and eggs."

"Will they make pancakes with peaches and blueberries in them at your friend's?"

"I'll ask, Gracey. I surely will."

23

It made the underpants of every editor in the city moist that Grace Savoy was out of jail. Reporters, photographers, and film crews were all over the St. Claire, which got its owners and developers on the phone with enough muscle that the NYPD permitted the detectives to resume their sidework.

Detectives Nucifora, Dunlop, and Welby were back in the lobby, and uniforms with relatives in high places were at the entrances. Stanley Antopol had snagged a way onto the detail and was on Rook's floor because he had worked it before as part of the rooftop job. He gave a nod as Lucas came out of his apartment with the old man.

Rook took Gracey off at the fourth floor, down the fire stairs and out the basement. The Japanese girl from Channel 5 was coming up the street with her people. She recognized Rook, which got her a look that would have reminded her of Hiroshima if she had any culture left, but at least was enough to convince her to keep on going.

Joe Oren could see that Lucas was working, so he let him be in the back booth and served up the pancakes with blueberries and peaches for the old man and ham and eggs for Rook without conversation. Jeanie went over to fill up their coffee cups.

"That man is blind," she said when she came back into the kitchen. "Blind and wearing *Heaven Sent*. I know the scents, Daddy, from getting ready to go to the Fashion Institute."

"He's working."

"The blind man?"

"Lucas is, Jeanie." Her father looked at his watch. "You have class soon?"

"I have another half hour here. Right, Sam?" she said.

"Don't be missing school," said the cook. "Especially to be spying on a man doing his job."

Joe held out his hand for his daughter's apron.

"Table seven said they wanted a side of grits," said Jeanie.

"I got that," answered her father.

"Sorry," said Jeanie. "I'll be leaving from the front door. Kisses."

Joe Oren handled the rest of Rook's meal, which included two orders of sausages for the old man, who turned out to be blind and probably not an old man at all. " 'Hot cakes and sausage, make them nice and brown,' " said Grace Savoy. "Ernie Kovacs said that. Then he married Edie Adams and died. She did cigar commercials."

"Very interesting," Lucas said. "Keep your voice down."

She did a very convincing baritone and kept quiet until they left.

Grace did her blind routine long enough to get a cab when they got outside.

"Not a good idea to give up on the old man thing," Lucas told her. "You're who you're pretending to be or whatever only until you're in the lawyer's office."

"Then I tell the truth, the whole truth, so help me, Warren G. Phelps."

"Something like that."

They had to wait when they got to Phelps' office, which was not uncommon. Rook looked through the magazines while Grace went in to change. She had the Andrea Thompson look when she came out.

A black girl showing a hint of her thong came out of one of the side offices and took them to the conference room across the hall.

"Judge Schwarzman will be with you shortly," she said.

"We're here for Warren Phelps," Rook told her.

"Of course," she answered. "He'll be joining you."

"We got a whole convention here. Warren, this judge, and that Felix Gavilan, shyster pimp to the stars, was here."

"Is that musk his? Actually there's two scents. The other is equally obscene."

"Ricky and Lucy. Felix represents the relative of the dead prick, Dwight Graves, who deserved what he got," said Lucas.

"It's not right to speak ill of the dead, Lucas. Especially dead pricks, which I don't really know that much about except I made one on your roof."

Warren G. Phelps, Esquire came out of his office accompanied by a white-haired man wearing gold-rimmed glasses and a two-thousand-dollar suit accented by a swan pin in the lapel. They all went into a conference room on the right.

The man offered a firm, but cool handshake. His cufflinks were also gold swans. "Jake Schwarzman, no T."

Lucas thought about cracking wise about maybe he lost the "T" when Warren added his phony middle initial. "Your girl said you're a judge."

"I was. Now I enjoy the pleasures and vagaries of private practice," said Schwarzman.

Vagaries, one of those billable, bullshit lawyer words. Lucas wondered what had gotten him off the bench, but from his confidence and clothes, it appeared to be big success.

"Warren has been kind enough to allow us to chat here while he and Ms. Savoy consult in his office," said Schwarzman.

"So I'm guessing it's not a good idea that I'm in there with her?" Lucas asked.

"Not a good idea," said Phelps. "There are issues of conflicts of interest, which is why I have asked Jake to meet with you."

"About what, gents?" said Rook. "I already have a lawyer, don't I?"

"I think you should discuss your personal injury claim with him, Lucas. It's Jake's specialty, not mine."

"If you say so."

"I do," said Phelps. "Now if you'll accompany me, Ms. Savoy, we'll be going to my office." Warren Phelps reached for her arm.

"Okey-dokey," she said. "But don't touch the merchandise."

Judge Schwarzman waited for them to leave.

"Warren has told me a lot about you," he said. "And has given me a thumbnail of your situation. I think I can help you."

"I'm listening, Judge."

"Grace is being represented by Warren in her criminal matter, as you know. A civil action has been filed on behalf of Detective Graves' estate by Felix Gavilan, whom I believe you are familiar with."

"I know him."

The lawyer took a sip of water. "Under 213-B, that action may be delayed until after the conclusion of any criminal proceedings against Ms. Savoy, which is what I would have done. Incidentally, Grace may or may not have separate counsel in the civil matter assigned by the carrier for her tenant's insurance policy. Such counsel will likely represent her under a reservation of rights. In any case, my surmise is that Warren will be filing a counterclaim on Ms. Savoy's behalf against Graves' estate and the City of New York for intentional and negligent infliction of emotional distress. I expect also a Section 11 action for worker's compensation contribution, and somewhere down the road a 601 Joinder."

Lucas stretched his bad leg. "Whatever all that means. And where does that leave us?"

"If I did represent you," said Schwarzman, "I would bring an action against the hotel, their holding company, I believe it's Argyle LLC, their development company, Mr. Graves' estate, and of course, his employer."

"I got a problem with suing the NYPD."

"Of course you do. I understand that. Then I ask for a 602 Consolidation 'for joint trial on all matters in issue.' If we're successful, which I believe we might very well be, we will have the defendants with the deep pockets chasing themselves."

Rook poured himself a glass of water. "601, 602, 'vagaries.' How can I resist? What rate are you talking about?"

"A contingency fee of thirty percent as a professional courtesy. I will attend any hearings on Ms. Savoy's criminal matter if we agree that is necessary, at a discounted rate of four hundred per hour."

"Costs come off first," said Rook. "Any referral fee to Warren is out of your end. What you all do with Felix is not my business. You don't collect on my civil case, I don't owe you any four hundreds."

Schwarzman handed over one of his cards. "My girl will get the fee agreement out to you. Call me Jake."

"Not 'The Swan'? I read the papers."

"Kind of over the top, but that's what they do. Jake is fine. Or Judge is fine, too."

"Sure," said Rook.

"Please do not discuss litigation matters with anyone," said Schwarzman. "Now if you'll excuse me, I have a matter back at my office. Very pretty woman, Ms. Savoy is."

"Swan-like?" Lucas said.

"Perhaps," said Schwarzman. The judge got up like he was on some decent exercise program and they shook hands.

Rook went back into the waiting room and looked through the magazines. The legalese bullshit and the sitting around was making him drowsy. He checked his watch and when out into the hall to use the gent's. Fancy building you don't have to ask for a key.

When he came back in, he checked with the receptionist, who checked with the secretary, who came out to show she was wearing a thong. Well-spoken piece of brown sugar, it's the right thing to do.

"I am not permitted to interrupt Warren, but I can check on Abaccus to see how much time he has blocked out."

"Appreciate it." She's calling him Warren, he's tapping that ass. Well, good for Warren G. Phelps and goodbye to asking her to show him that g-string up close.

She came back in a moment. Maybe a hint of fresh lip gloss, which gave Lucas a hint of hard-on. "I'm afraid they'll be another forty-five minutes," she said. "If you'd like to go out, I'll call you on your cell if they break earlier."

"Going out would be a good idea, Miss Legal Assistant Lady."

"My name is Serena."

"That's it?" Rook said.

"That's it," she said with a smile that didn't mean anything else. "I'll call as soon as they adjourn."

"Adjourn?" Rook wrote his cell number. "Let me know when they're also done."

A pain in the ass, all this lawyer shit, which means you need to smack somebody or get a shine from Jimbo Turner. Lucas took a cab over to his stand.

A soft man in a pretend bush hat was getting his pretend boots done and complaining about a half dozen things. The shine-man finished him up and used the whisk broom on his customer's coat and hat.

Lucas got up on to the stand. "How ya doin', Mr. Turner?"

"Not bad for a diabetic, half-blind white shineman." He leaned in close. "Going to blood them up a bit," Jimbo said.

"You're the boss."

Jimbo Turner took a bottle of wash from the bottom drawer and cleaned Rook's shoes.

"Man's always going on about something that just got off my stand. Rich as he is. Pretty wife. They own some leasing company or something. He's always complaining about something. And he don't know one-tenth what the world can be doin' to you."

"I would think not, Mr. Turner. Now with your kind permission, I'm going to doze up here for five minutes or so."

"You take whatever you need, my friend. Give me a chance to put the oxblood on, and then change them laces you got double knotted."

The shineman worked the color in with his fingertips and then took out his brushes, clickety-clack and then the saddle soap and the brushes again. He took the rag from his apron pocket and brought up the shine while he popped the rag. Jimbo finished off with a piece of nylon stocking so Rook's shoes shined like glass and put in the laces, pulling them tight and doing the double knots.

Lucas opened his eyes. "I feel good as new," he said.

"Good enough to bring an old white shineman some Jersey reds and bag of sweet corn?"

"That I will," said Lucas Rook.

Rook's phone rang as he was getting down.

"They're just breaking up," Serena said.

"And us?"

"I'll tell Warren you are on your way," she said.

23

You're going to meet with the lawyer who got you out from under putting a couple into somebody's head, you bring a pound of corned beef. Especially if you need a fat and nitrate infusion yourself and he's also representing a friend of yours who's in the jackpot for keeping you from being dead.

Serena could smell the deli as Rook came in.

"I'm a vegan," she said as she walked Lucas to Warren Phelps' office.

"Of course you are," he told her. "Too complicated. I don't like complicated."

Phelps came out.

"A godsend, the deli," he said. "I'll knock a couple hundred dollars off of one of your bills some day. Let's go into the conference room and make it smell like corned beef for the next week."

"I can smell corned beef a mile away," said Grace Savoy.

"Of course you can. And hear it too," said Phelps.

"Kiss, kiss, Lucas," she said. "We've been having oodles of fun."

"Oodles," said Phelps. "Shall we adjourn to our repast?"

Serena spread out the corned beef, rye bread, and the rest of the goodies on the conference room table and then left to wash her hands.

"Reminds me when I had the 'we're getting married' talk with my late father-in-law," said Warren. "I'm marrying his daughter who's fifteen years younger. I'm married before. I'm not of the

Catholic faith. I'm from New York, which in his Indiana mind means I'm Jewish." He took a bite of one of the sour tomatoes. "He indicates he has questions, which naturally I assume relate to the various differences and so on. He proposes one interrogatory and one only."

"And that interrogatory is?" asked Lucas.

" 'How much is corned beef a pound?' he asks me. I do not jest."

Serena came in with a tray of Diet Cokes and a sparkling water for her boss.

"Let me make the sandwiches. It will be a teddy bear's picnic," said Grace.

"You think we're teddy bears?" asked Warren.

"You two are," she said. "I killed a man."

"A teddy bear who feared for her life and the life of her friend. And who could not see," said the attorney. "And is not to say that again. Do you understand that, Grace?"

"Sho do," she said.

"How we doing, Counselor?" asked Lucas.

"We're doing just fine. I think they're going to have their hands full at the preliminary hearing."

"The DA must have their panties in a knot they let the grand jury run out," said Lucas.

Grace Savoy tucked a dangling piece of corned beef into her mouth. " 'Hands full, panties in a knot,' I like that. It's nice. Not to mention my face full of meat."

Rook was used to that kind of talk from her and let it go. Warren shook his head.

"We shall see why they effectively waived the grand jury," said Phelps. "They had their 144 hours to get their evidence in, which they didn't. Which is why we have Ms. Savoy ROR."

"Released on her own recognizance," she said.

"On a cop homicide?" asked Lucas.

"We had no opposition to my application, Lucas."

"Right, like where am I going? Meaning not that I couldn't, but millions of people have seen this beautiful face."

"Exactly," said Phelps.

"Cha-ching," said Gracey.

"I don't understand," said Warren.

"That was the billing thing," she said.

"He's worth it," said Rook as he dabbed a spot of mustard on his shirt.

"I appreciate that," said Phelps. "In any case, the wheels of Justice are turning, and somewhat like a merry-go-round. I got a call from the section chief, Vecchione. You know him?"

"Started out on the lobster shift, doing arraignments at three o'clock in the morning," said Lucas. "Now he's running big cases. I was on a couple of homicides with him. What do they say, 'tough, but fair,' which means he tried to break the bad guys' balls, which was fine with me."

"And also he's smart," said Warren. "For Ms. Savoy, that's good because I'll be very surprised that he's going to prejudice what he might have with what he doesn't have. And here, that's premeditation."

"I did that once," said Grace Savoy. "And past life regression. It turns out I was…"

"We have to stay on track here," said the lawyer. "Vecchione can show that Grace goes and gets the gun. He can't show what her intent was since she didn't know who was on the roof and so on, because she can't see. Right, Grace?"

"Right, sir. I *comprende.*"

"Therefore he drops the Murder One charge so the judge and the jury don't turn on him and his whole case goes south. What Vecchione does is threaten us with manslaughter and hopes that we take a deal on involuntary."

"And what do we do?" said Grace. "Other than 'the not-guilty by the fact that I'm cuckoo' thing, which I told you I do not want to do."

"That's the weapon we threaten him with," said Phelps. "In the meantime, we prepare."

"What do you want me to do?" asked Lucas.

"The grand jury has run out and you haven't been noticed for the preliminary hearing yet, Lucas, so it's alright we spoke about old times for a few minutes today. But I don't want it hanging out there I was interfering with their witness. In any case, I'll be reviewing your statement to the police, Ms. Savoy's, and whatever somebody can get me on Detective Dwight Graves."

Grace got up from her chair. "Are you going to testify against me, Lucas Rook?"

"He makes our case, Ms. Savoy, not theirs. He hurts them, not you. Please relax."

"I can only say what I saw, Gracey."

"That's more than I can," she said.

"Then don't worry," said Rook.

"I feel better," she said. "I think I'll take a pee now."

"Clever lady," the lawyer said when she left the room. "But clever's not always the best thing." He took a bite of his sandwich. "Especially if one appears to be so. We agree they have to charge Ms. Savoy because they have a detective shot dead on that roof, and a black detective at that. Then again, you're their only witness and what you have to say gives them nothing."

"Maybe it's what I don't have to say they're after, Warren."

Phelps buzzed his secretary to hold Grace until he finished with Rook. "Which is what?"

"That Graves was a dirty cop. Which is maybe why the grand jury got fouled up. Somewhere on the line somebody whispers in somebody's ear that there's something they don't want to see the light of day."

Phelps finished the rest of his corned beef. "It hurts the prosecution substantially that their dead black detective was dirty."

"My twin brother worked with Dwight."

"I understand." Phelps took the top piece of bread off the other half of his sandwich. "And likely the DA does too. But Vecchione's not going to risk losing any back cases. Any defense attorney worth his diploma would be all over getting convictions thrown out, regardless which detective…"

"So you need everything you can get on Graves?" Rook asked.

"Precisely." He poured himself some of the Diet Coke. "Anything about your brother is irrelevant in any case. I need a focus on Dwight Graves. Are we good with that? I can't have you doing or not doing anything to the detriment of Grace Savoy's defense."

"No problem," said Rook. "Now you better get your client back in here so you don't lose any billable time."

Phelps buzzed Gracey in. Her face looked different, brighter. "I look even happy, don't I?" she said. "It's amazing what some make-up and two good men can do. And I can do it all in the dark."

Warren Phelps got up and reached to take her hand. She kissed him on the cheek.

"We'll do fine here," the lawyer said.

"At your rates we better," she said.

Rook cabbed down to 166th Fifth Avenue. Manny was in the foyer, looking pretty good considering he had just got out of the joint and his head had cancer in it.

"You alright?" Lucas asked.

"Thanks for taking care of my kid. Talking to him and all."

"Sure, Emmanuel, sure."

There was the usual crap upstairs. Crap mail, crap phone messages. Ray Tuzio, when he wasn't sitting in his own crap because his mind had turned to crap, had said that the world was like a bag of crap on summer day, except when it wasn't. Then you could forget about the summer part.

Lucas got to work on the interim report and bill on the Circuit City job. A nice piece of change and it wasn't over yet, following up with both precincts and like that. Maybe he'd get something steady with them after they saw his handiwork. In the meantime, there was going to be a fee one way or another from digging Dwight Graves through the shit. How that was going to play out was something that he hadn't exactly figured out.

A knock on what would have been his outer door before the rent increase meant moving to an office without a waiting room. The cloying cologne preceded resplendent attorney Felix Gavilan, Esquire, with his cufflinks the size of clock radios and his Roly the size of a big screen TV. The lawyer's new "assistant" was posing like the tough guy.

"*Hola*, Lucas. It is so good to see you up and around. I understand we just missed each other at Warren's office."

"Sure, Felix. Aren't you going to introduce me to your new friend?"

"Enrique has no sense of humor, I'm afraid."

"Pity, pity. You're here to talk about you suing my friend, you know I got nothing to say. Besides, I might do something that could get me and Enrique doing the tango."

"Count on it," said Enrique with a heavy accent and just the hint of fag.

"Of course not, Lucas. We've done good business together. I wouldn't do anything to middle you for that reason alone, not to mention the Canons of Ethics."

"You don't have any calendars with you, Felix," said Rook. "So why in heaven's name are you gay caballeros paying me this surprise visit?"

The assistant took a half step forward. Rook stood up.

"Please, please," said Gavilan. "I only wanted to give you this, which has nothing at all to do with the fact that you witnessed anything."

He took the small box from Enrique. "Only my best clients get these. For promotional purposes only."

Lucas opened the box. Gold cufflinks with the scales of justice on one and Felix's face on the other.

"They don't match, counselor. I mean, you're the master of elegance, but shouldn't there be two of the same?"

"You think so?" said Gavilan. "I really don't, but then again, my taste is a bit more eclectic."

"Well, good for the two of you," said Lucas. "Now, we've got nothing else here, I've got some serious sleuthing to do."

The lawyer gave Enrique the look again and got another box, which he handed to Rook.

"This way you have two matching sets, Lucas," said Gavilan.

Rook underhanded the boxes to Enrique, who caught them both with his left hand. A queer for sure, but somebody who knows the bodyguard business.

"And now my Felix, *hasta la* something. And I hope your client gets zilch, which will be the case if I've got anything to with that."

"I hope not," said Gavilan. "I'm very good at what I do. You have my 800 number if you'd like some fine dining."

"I think I'll pass, Felix. Which is more than I can say about Enrique. So, *adios*, and don't let the *puerta* hit you on the way out."

24

Gavilan is out the door and another kind of pain in the ass shows up at the office not fifteen minutes after. Fat, buttery type.

"Already bought mine," Lucas told her.

"What's that?" said Vecchione's flunky.

"The thin mints, whatever. Them cookies you're selling."

"You're as funny as a heart attack. Oh, guess I shouldn't have said that. I'm from the district attorney's office. You've been served." She put the subpoena on his desk. "Don't be late."

Lucas dropped the papers in the trash can. "Don't let the door hit your ample ass on the way out, dearie."

So Karl Vecchione, Chief of the Homicide Unit, has decided to break balls, he didn't make a courtesy phone call. Maybe he forgot the couple of times his case got saved for him or even when he was starting and had to be told where to stand. Schwarzman would take care of that, and in the meantime he felt a case of amnesia coming on.

Lucas called down to the garage. Make a quick run out to check Tuze before things got busy. Check on Catherine too.

"What?" Rosen answered.

"Good way to treat your customers, answering the phone like that, Sidney."

"I love cars. I hate the people who own them, Lucas boy. With certain exceptions, of course."

"Going to be going out to the Home," Lucas told him. "I'll be by in about fifteen."

Lucas took the summons out of the circular file and called over to The Swan's office that he'd been served and for when. Leaving a message was good because a lawyer answers your call he charges you for that and the memo he dictates about it the same time. He works six minutes and one second, he's charging you four tenths of an hour, which is what you make a day. Rook called Catherine and got her answering machine, which she was finally smart enough to use a mechanical voice on instead of her own, which was an invitation to the bad guys.

Another knock at his door. There hadn't been this much commotion since Eddie Doyle blew his own self up with his homemade bomb filled with nails. It was Manny again. He had a gift in his hand. "Don't say no," he said.

"Appreciate it, Emmanuel. You'd do the same for me."

Maybe he would, maybe he wouldn't. But most likely Emmanuel wouldn't already be thinking about re-gifting the thing, which was likely going to happen.

The phone rang. It was Cat.

"It is so nice to hear your voice," she said.

"Now that I am up and around, I would like to take you out fancy."

"And when would that be, kind sir?"

He could hear her light a cigarette, but let it be.

"Got room on my dance card tonight," he told her.

"That soon? How about today? Like in a couple of hours. Comet's, the bookstore in Princeton, is closing and they're having a little get-together."

"I'll wear something presentable," said Lucas.

"I'll meet you there." She took another drag on her cigarette. "I love you," she said. "I'll meet you there at five."

Lucas checked his watch, which he wore on his right hand so somebody who thinks they know what's going on takes you for a southpaw. Call Owlsie to get what he needed set up and start some serious spadework on Dwight. Run over to see Tuze after midnight to catch the pretend nurses asleep, or first thing tomorrow morning if he stays over at Catherine's.

Owls Miksis still answering his own phone. You're talking about looking deep at a cop you don't talk about it over the phone, particularly with Jaluski and Internal Affairs been around.

"I got something for you," Rook said. "I can come out tomorrow."

"Wednesday night's better. Unless it can't wait."

"Tomorrow's better. What time we talking, Owlsie?"

"Anytime after eight. You beat the traffic that way."

"Nine," said Rook.

"Nine. See you then," said Miksis. "Knock like usual so I don't shoot at you."

Lucas stopped off for Mexican on the way back to his apartment. "You got anything with beans and cheese?" he asked the girl behind the counter.

"We got stuff with cheese and beans," said the assistant manager when he saw who it was.

"I'll take that, Orlando. Everything good?"

"Good, good. You want something with chicken in it, beef? I charge you the same."

"Appreciate that. I'll keep my eye out for illegals tunneling in."

"Don't look too hard."

"Gotcha," said Lucas.

He took a seat where he could watch the cash register and the front door. Orlando sent the girl over with some flan.

"Nice," said Rook.

"I don't think so," she said.

"I meant the caramel custard here, dear. I'm not partial myself to girls with hardware stuck through their eyelids."

"Whatever," she said and she made sure that his middle-aged eyes saw how nice her ass was that he wasn't going to get within a mile of even if he were twenty years younger.

Orlando sent over a ton of food. That would make the thing at the bookstore perfect, they're going to be putting out little tea-things you could eat a dozen of, it wouldn't even make a dent.

Lucas gave a five to the girl at the register and nothing for the smart ass waitress who could eat his leftovers. You start taking food home, you're halfway there to saving paper bags and rubber bands. He went back to the St. Claire. Maybe someday he'll say where he used to live, maybe, or it'll be where Warren G. Phelps and The Swan get him a condo. Detective Antopol was in the lobby enjoying the sanctioned side job.

"Looks like you're golden," Lucas told him.

"I wish. My ex got me working here on my RDO, annual whatever. I mean here or wherever, so I don't have to be eating no dog food. *Alimony pendente lite* they call it, so her fucking attorney and her can live the life of Riley. Not that they're together from what I know. I mean except the way they're taking me to the cleaners."

"Nice," said Rook. Stanley's being a drama queen here, which means he's about to get worked real good. "You got that too many double shifts look, partner," said Lucas.

"You got that right. But I ain't got no choice. It's not like I'm doing this side work so I can go to Aruba or whatever. Now it goes though the PD. They take all the taxes out, the wife's lawyer gets my W-2 or whatever. Jaluski fucked this up good."

Now we're talking. "You get a break here, Stanley, we should talk, maybe I got something for you. Nothing about me getting it up on that roof or whatever. Us both be in that court case the way it's going."

"You buying, I'm flying," Antopol told him.

They went around the corner for a pitcher so he could take the conversation where it needed to go.

Stanley took a long drink and reached for his smokes. "You mind, I mean your chest and all?"

For where this was going to go, Lucas didn't mind at all. "Knock yourself out."

Antopol fired up a Marlboro and palmed it so nobody would give him any shit.

"How you doing, Rook?"

"I could do without being shot up. The trial of that blind girl's going to be a circus. But at least you're getting paid court time, Stan. I'm getting squat."

"Never had time for Dwight Graves anyhow, haughty mother-fucker." Antopol took another long drink of beer.

"His people are suing the PD, me, the blind lady."

"You're shitting me."

"Suing the Department and a blind woman," said Lucas.

"You got lawyers, right?"

"I got The Swan."

"Then you got it knocked, Rook. The Swan's number one."

Antopol finished his glass and poured another.

"They looking for anybody to do side work, I mean any of the lawyers, I'm good to go." A long drag on the cigarette. "I can get shit nobody can."

"Jaluski'll crucify you they find out you're working on a case like this."

"Fuck them cheese-eaters. You let them pay my alimony. Plus there's no way they're picking up I'm doing whatever."

"You still got the lawyers paying you, it gets written down. Your wife, IAB, whoever, wants to jam you up, you got a paper trail, unless you're paid cash." Lucas got up. "I got to take my two-beer piss."

Antopol started another smoke. Lucas could see the hook was in when he got back from the gents'.

"You help me with that, Rook, I help you, your friend, the blind girl. I'm there for both of you. And maybe I can eat something but Alpo."

"We can do this, Stanley. Her lawyer's goin' to be wanting all kinds of shit on Graves. And I can work with it so it's not getting back to you."

"No problem, I'll run his 5's, his 6's. His 7 and 5/8's. Whatever it takes."

"Old stuff, new stuff."

"No problem."

"Cash money, Stan. And I'll see that you don't got to go through nobody but me."

"Appreciate that, Rook, I do. Christ, my daughter's orthodontist bill would choke a horse."

Rook handed over the $100 he had in his wallet. "So you'll know I'm on the level about this."

"I know you are, Rook. Listen, you need me to dig the fucker up, I will."

"One thing, DG and my brother worked some jobs…"

"Kirk? No problem. I hear ya. You get what I get. I do with it what you want, good?" said Antopol.

"Good," said Rook and he poured them each another beer.

25

Sid Rosen was arguing with a genuine bitch in her three-hundred-dollar running suit when Lucas got to the garage. She was yelling and he was not budging an inch.

"My husband is a federal magistrate," she said over and over. "And we will not be gouged or extorted. Your bill is absolutely outrageous."

"And you're not getting your car back. You signed the estimate, I did the work."

"The insurance is to pay you. And besides, my husband, who you will know is a federal magistrate, said…"

"Tell His Honor that if he wants you to have your toy back he can send the marshals down. In the meantime I am asserting my garageman's lien and asking you to leave."

"You'll be hearing from my husband."

"And you'll be paying your bill before you get your car back or it will be going up for auction."

"Well, I never…" she said, turning to leave and almost bumping into Lucas Rook.

"I believe that, Madame," Rosen said on her way out.

"She aggravating you, Sidney?"

"On the contrary, Lucas, I'm congratulating myself for not taking her shit, not giving her her car, and not calling her a cunt."

"Commendable on all counts."

"I don't know why women should be so outraged about the word. The etymology is clear."

"Bugs, right?"

"Words. As you know, Lucas boy, because we have had this conversation twice before, one is the study of words, *etymology*. The other, *entomology*, is the study of insects."

"Which should be *ant*omology?"

"Correct." He wiped his hands on the towel on his desk. "And we are discussing *cuntomology*."

"I thank you for your teaching, kind sir. Now, I do need a vehicle."

"The Mercury or the Avanti, which by the way I had another call from that Currerri, who still wants to buy it."

"Kirk's car it is then, Sidney."

"You give me a hand, we'll have you ready to roll. In the meantime, while you're helping me bury Mrs. Cunty's Volvo in the back and get your coupe out, contemplate that the origin of the word 'cunt' is from the Old Norse *kanta*, which by the way you would not have learned from the book you have yet to return to me."

The garageman took a set of keys off the board. "You going Italian or Chinese, bring me something back."

"A bookstore, Sidney. This place in Princeton's closing."

"Bring me something from there," said the garageman.

"A book, or you talking some kind of souvenir?"

"Either. Now let me get you out of here so I can go pick up my best friend at the vet before he thinks I've abandoned him, which was actually to get dipped and his nails cut. You got to be careful with that, their blood's so close to the surface."

"I'll see if they have a book on cunts *and* German shepherds."

"Perfect," said Rosen.

"Perfect," said Rook.

They moved the cars around and Lucas was on his way to meet Catherine. You had to get to the Holland Tunnel earlier and earlier to avoid the rush-hour gridlock, which now started before four and then spread down the Turnpike so that getting to Exit 9 was like getting crosstown. EZ Pass made a big difference, but you use that, it's going to bite you in the ass that somebody's going to be able to put you where they want you to be.

The traffic was good down to US 1 and Washington Road, so Lucas was at Comet's with twenty minutes to spare. There was a line outside of the bookstore already so he sat in his car and picked up his calls. The only one worth the time was Felix Gavilan doing his fawning shit with the menace underneath. "Fawning," another gift from Sid.

He was listening to the message a second time for laughs when another call came through.

"I'm running a little bit late," said Catherine Wren.

"There's a line already."

"You're in it, I hope."

"I don't do waiting in line, Cat. You know that."

"Okay. We'll butt in. You can arrest somebody."

"Jack them too?"

"Hijacking. I like that," she said.

"Blackjack, I meant. But we can hijack them too."

"See you soon," she told him. "Love ya."

Catherine Wren was another twenty minutes, which meant the doors were open and the place filled. Lots of tweedy types and the requisite number of lesbians, gays, and dogs with kerchiefs.

A black chick with dreadlocks came over. "I'm glad you're here. So's Ross, but as you can see he's got his hands full."

Rook figured she meant the light-skinned man behind the register in the Daytona 500 tee-shirt.

"This is my gentleman friend, Lucas Rook," Catherine said.

"You don't look like a fascist pig at all," said the girl.

"I'm in disguise," he told her.

"Feel free to look around. Everything's half off."

"It must make you sad," said Cat. "You and Ross."

"Not really. We're moving to Spokane to open up there."

Lucas walked over to the pet section. He found a perfect title, *The Vegan Diet for the Active Dog*, and browsed for something for Catherine. A couple of old queens, one with long hair the color of an Irish setter, cruised him. Lucas minded his manners and browsed on. A copy of *The Quintessential Woman's Guide for Peace and Harmony*. Too bad there was nothing in Old Norse.

Cat had her hands full. Books on art, politics, flowers, running.

"It's a sin they're moving," she said. "Politics, it's always about politics. Which reminds me, how is Grace doing?"

"You're a little ahead of me here."

"If you don't serve coffee, nobody comes in, Lucas. Somebody wouldn't give them the permits, which is why they have to move."

"That's what lawyers are for, Catherine."

"They wouldn't do that. They believe lawyers are the endemic cause of what's wrong with our society."

"I don't know what 'endemic' means, but if it's anything like 'epidemic,' they're right."

They were up at the register. Ross shook hands with both of them. "We appreciate you coming."

"We wouldn't miss it," said Catherine.

"And I appreciate that. We'll be thinking of you," he told him.

"Right," said Rook.

They paid and went back outside.

"No wine and cheese. I thought we'd have wine and cheese," Lucas said.

"They're leaving. I'm not really good at goodbyes." She put her arm through his. "Let's not have any more of those, Lucas."

"And I won't jack anybody, unless they really need it."

"Let's go home," Catherine said.

He followed her in his fiberglass coupe. She poured them each a glass of wine when they got to her place. Then she wept. Maybe about Ross. Maybe about him, maybe about the wounds that scarred his chest. "My heart," she said. "My life's love." She kissed him. And when she was ready, they went into her room.

At two o'clock Rook's cell phone rang. It was the Policeman's Home.

"I've got to go," he told Catherine. "Ray Tuzio's fading fast."

"I'm coming too," she said.

He started to argue, but grabbed his keys.

"Come on," he said, "but don't say nothing."

Rook pushed the Avanti hard, but by the time he got there, the man who had taught him about the street and saved his life coming through the door with his riot gun was dead.

"Where's his Aviators?" he asked the nurse in charge.

"His what?"

"His sunglasses. I'll give you until the count of five to give them up."

"They're right here in the drawer beside his bed."

Lucas put them on Ray Tuzio. "You can roll now, Tuze," he said.

The poor bastard in the next bed got up and was peeing in the corner. Rook grabbed him hard.

"Don't you got no respect?" he said. "He was ten times the man you ever were."

The man fell down.

Catherine went to get the nurse. Lucas wrapped his friend in the blanket and lifted him up.

"What are you doing?" said the supervisor, who came in with Cat.

"I'm taking Raymond Joseph Tuzio so he gets the proper funeral he deserves and you don't cut him up for parts."

"I know you're upset, but the patient must be pronounced. Now please, allow us to…"

Rook walked at him hard, Tuzio weighing hardly nothing and Lucas opening up his jacket so to show his .45.

"They said they would move your friend to a private room," said Catherine. "We could sit with him."

"I'm taking him over to Evans' myself. You want, they can call you a cab or I'll come back."

"I'm coming with you," she said.

Lucas Rook carried Ray Tuzio outside and put him in the back seat of the black Avanti coupe. Rook let Catherine put her hand on his shoulder as they drove through the night in the car that was his twin brother's a thousand years ago.

26

A cop like Raymond Tuzio is getting laid out, there's going to be a dozen good guys there to see him off. Those who rode with him, went through doors with him. Putting on their dark suits and cop's shoes to do it right. Some were there because they thought they should be. Then there were the assholes who just wanted a change of duty for the day, and of course, the pencil-neck brass from One Police Plaza.

Arthur leaned over to the boss next to him. "Them guineas always talking about when Joe Petrossino got it, there were a quarter of a million at his funeral. So that was what, a hundred years ago. I keep hearing that. I don't see two hundred fifty here, let alone two hundred fifty thousand."

"You ask me, he was part of the Black Hand himself from what I hear, Petrossino was."

Lucas Rook came in carrying the casket of his dead friend with McCullagh across from him and the rest of the pallbearers from the Columbus Benevolent Association.

Jeanie Oren was there with her father, Joe, and she reached out to touch Rook's sleeve as he walked by. Mark Johnson, Nucifora, Johnny Morris, Antopol and Carillo were there as much for themselves as they were for Tuzio or Lucas Rook. So were a dozen more gold shields who were on the job long enough not to be carpet munchers, minorities or the like. Lieutenant Jaluski and his flunky showed. No doubt to see who was there, which should have been enough to get their vehicle at least fucked up if it wasn't that it might be the wrong day to do the right thing.

Father Corsinite's service was long. So was the three-mile ride from Bayside to Mount Saint Mary's to put Tuze in the ground. The procession that came over to the cemetery and the assholes from One Police Plaza making sure their top of the lines went after the hearse in order of the rank they had sucked cock to earn.

The lunch was back in Bayside at Biggica's, where the bosses stayed only long enough to show their braid. Arthur had three drinks, which was twice as long as it took for his welcome to wear out. Antopol gave Rook the sign and they went outside, where he handed over an envelope which just as well could have been a boost to pay for the flowers or whatever, but was a raft of shit on Dwight Graves.

Stanley waited for something in return.

"Didn't think you worked so fast," said Lucas.

"I got orthodonture to pay for and the alimony."

"Tomorrow."

"Tomorrow is good," said Antopol. "You got Tuze to see to." He walked away when Biggica came over.

"The luncheon's mine," Russ said. "And the Benevolent says there's enough to pay the funeral parlor and the headstone."

"I got the stone," said Rook.

"I hear you. And we'll make sure his name goes up on the memorial in Albany." He started away and then came back. "Evans' tells me Ray's sunglasses went with him like you said. You need me, you call me."

When Biggica said that he meant it, which is probably why he was not one of those braided-up shit-for-brains who were eating his food and drinking the wine from his upstate vines.

Rook went back towards the men's room then out the side door. Arthur and Stratton were just pulling out.

"He was a good cop," said Stratton.

"Fuck you both," said Rook. "And now you two can get back to stroking each other off."

Lucas took his Mercury back to Rosen's garage. Sidney had something meaningful to say, and handed him a poetry book about loss by Shirley Adelman.

Rook went back to his apartment and looked at the shit that Antopol had dug up. Case summaries, arrest reports. Some of it was bad shakedowns, and two bad shoots made right. Nothing about Kirk. Plenty about the scumbag partner, Banks. Some stink on Hy Gromek that a pretty good-sized policy bank got the eternal Pasadena. But Hy's shit was going to get re-buried.

Then Lucas settled in to getting hammered. A bad idea for a cop to get loaded by himself after a funeral, but it was okay now that he had some mean work to get after. The phone rang twice. Once from Valerie that she was off at eleven and another from Catherine Wren to see if he was alright and that she wished he had allowed her to go to the funeral with him.

"No you don't," he told her.

"Yes I do, I could…"

"You could see me tomorrow instead of now, which is not very good."

"Can I do anything for you, Lucas? I know the two of you were close."

"I'm good."

"I'm close to you, Lucas. I'm close to you right now."

"Fine, Cat. I appreciate that. I'll call you tomorrow."

He hung up and poured himself another drink and made himself a salami sandwich to counteract the alcohol. There was movement out on the patio. It was his neighbor coming over in one of her crazy cape things. If it was one of the more annoying Grace Savoys that knocked on his slider, she was going to have to take her blind ass back home.

Gracey came in and sat down without a word. She pulled her knees up and covered herself all up with the black silk wrap. She sat silent.

"You want a drink, Grace?"

"And a piece of salami, please," she said.

There was a knock on the apartment door.

"I'll get it," she said.

"No you won't."

Lucas Rook took his .45 off the mantelpiece and went down the short hallway. It was a basket of fruit from Wingy Rosenzweig.

"Take this home, Grace. Me and produce are enemies."

"Thank you," she said. "I can smell the grapes, the apples…" she stopped.

They sat there for a while, Rook with his automatic in his hand and his blind neighbor wanting a cigarette. Grace went out on to the patio to smoke, then came back in.

"You could have done that in here."

"I didn't want to disturb…" ·

"The fruit. They'll be alright. In fact, give me one."

"They're menthols. I didn't know you smoked, Lucas."

Everybody did. Especially cops. Sometimes it's the only thing for you to do except pissing in a jar in a midnight stakeout. "I was just going to fiddle with it," he told her.

Gracey pantomimed like she was playing a violin.

"Don't," he told her.

"I'm nervous," she said. "Scared. I know you are grieving, but I'm frightened. My preliminary hearing's coming up."

"You got the best there is, Gracey."

The phone rang. It was Warren Phelps. "My condolences, Lucas."

"I was just talking about you."

"Good, I trust."

"To my neighbor."

"Her preliminary hearing is moved to Friday. Their office is going to be plenty busy. There's a flurry of motions for them to deal with, starting with my 180-30."

"Whatever that means."

"It means the poor outclassed, overmatched, underpaid public servant's trying to reconcile the fact that I asked for a determination whether the felony complaint should be dismissed and a misdemeanor filed with the court in lieu of."

"Mumbo jumbo, Counselor. But it's what you do best. What I do best I'm doing, so you'll be hearing from that friend of mine."

"Of course. Tell Ms. Savoy not to worry."

Grace had turned her cape inside-out so that when Lucas turned around she was wrapped in white.

"It is the color of mourning in Asia," she said.

"Ray was Italian, Gracey."

"Out of respect," she said. "And I'm covering all bases. When I go home, I'll be putting on a *burkha* and a *tallis*."

Lucas thought of telling her that should be now, but went into the kitchen to start the mellowing-out process with a couple of beers.

"You want to come over for dinner?" Grace asked him.

"I didn't know that you cooked."

"I don't really," she said. "But I figured you're hungry enough to come over to my place, I could order in, or if you wanted to you could let me take you out."

"Warren G. Phelps said not to worry," Lucas said.

Grace lit a cigarette. "Easy for you to say, when you can see what's going on. I can't remember, I mean I can, but I can't. I can tell from your voice that you are not lying or at least, believe what you say. Also…"

"Hold on, Gracey. I don't want you to have to lie about what we've talked about."

She flicked an ash into her hand. "Okay, okay. Let me change into something less ceremonial and you can take me out for something to eat. I'll pretend we're on a date so I won't think about any-body locking me away for the rest of my life."

"Two conditions," he told her. "You've got to ratchet it down, Gracey, and we have to be back by eight. I have an appointment."

She got up. "Another damsel in distress?"

"Business, Gracey."

"Then I'll not dawdle in putting on my 'back-by-eight' face."

"And one more thing, Grace. I'm not eating anything served by somebody showing their nipple rings."

They settled for Tex-Mex on Hudson Street. Good food, cold beer. Grace Savoy insisted on paying and he let her.

"I feel better, Lucas Rook. Not so shaky inside," she said after.

"That's good," he told her.

She stood tight against him in the elevator and breathed on his neck.

"I make you hard, don't I?" she said.

"You do, Gracey. But you're my neighbor and I've got work to do."

"Only if you kiss me at my door."

They had kissed twice before, which was once too much.

He kissed her on the cheek. "If you need me, you can get me on my cell. Meanwhile, your lawyer and your friend told you not to worry. So don't."

"I will," she said. "But only a little, and that's until the Xanax kicks in." Grace unlocked the door, then turned back around. "Thank you, Lucas."

Rook went inside and called Owls Miksis to say he was on his way. He could sense, then hear somebody following him to Rosen's garage. Rook stepped into the shadows as the alley turned. The pus bag was going to get it fast and then Owls was going to get the dirt on Dwight Graves to pass along to Warren Phelps. It felt good to be alive.

27

Somebody's following you down an alley, it's 10 to 1 some street scum wanting to rip you off to feed their habit. Now because of DG getting what he deserved, which was being blown away up on that roof, you can't discount it's somebody half-connected to that, particularly the way the "brothers" were acting at the hospital.

Surprise, surprise, it is the lover boy from the Econolodge at Englewood again. This gets him a Glock jammed into the back of his head and then he's snatched into the shadows.

"Don't you move, don't you fucking breathe," Rook said.

"Fuck you, fuck you. I don't care what you do."

Lucas Rook spun him around and pressed the barrel of the .45 into his throat.

"You do, lover boy. I see you again, I am going to kill you. Or maybe I'm going to hurt you bad so you can't talk and see."

"Do it! Do it! I lost my job, my family. I'm being sued. It's in the newspapers."

"About your little ass play? They talking how what's-her-name's riding you with that strap-on?"

The mope shook his head.

"I take it that's a 'no,' but I can fix that for you so that's part of the story. So why don't you just go home and ride this out. You seem to like that anyway. You don't do that, I'm going to see everybody sees the tape I got you taking that dildo up your hairy ass and loving it. Then I'm going to hurt you in a way you're not going to like."

Rook kneed him in the balls. "Now run along and go home and change your panties."

Then he went over to the garage to get the Merc and run out to the Bronx to see Owlsie, which he doesn't talk about because that means giving Sidney knowledge about Miksis, who is how Warren Phelps gets the info on Dwight. And you never put a friend in the middle, unless it's life or death.

The ride out to 159th Street took less time than Owlsie to go on about the polo grounds and the Giants, which he always did. Today it was about Wes Westnum and Johnny Antonelli and somebody he called Mandrake the Magician.

Lucas gave Owls what Antopol had given him on Dwight Graves, talking slow so Miksis could get it down in his own hand. The bad cop stuff, which included a connection with Etillio, and big money from some busts gone missing. There was some other undocumented stuff on Dwight's private life, which was that he liked to hurt his women. Antopol had a couple of names which might or might not have been accurate, only one address.

Lucas Rook drove back into the city after spending almost two hours with Owls Miksis, who kept saying "Yeah, yeah," as he took notes, which Rook would get to Phelps in the morning. "I should learn to type."

He stopped on the way back to his apartment to pick up life's essentials, which were toilet paper, beer, some more beer and two packs of pork roll. No way with the blood he lost, the cholesterol isn't down. If not, Docs Fenton and DiBona can play jump ball about who gets to tell him he's being an asshole. Speaking of which, Cholly the shrink was going to have to wait a little bit longer again. But just to make it kosher for Catherine, he placed a call.

"I'm calling to schedule," Lucas told Cholly's message machine and hung up. Mission accomplished. Then he turned the ringer off on his phone and lay down on the sofa to rest, one of the lovely holdovers from getting shot.

Rook lay there and tried not to fall asleep. Just take it easy, get warm, charge the batteries. It was morning when he woke up. One call was waiting for him. Cholly calling back to inquire whether he wished the kind of appointment that you can keep or the kind of appointment that you don't.

Gracey's preliminary hearing was coming up, which meant there were two days to do some more spade work. Sid would like that, "spade work" on Dwight Graves. Irony was one of Rosen's favorite things next to getting his crank yanked by any subdivision of the universe of Asian girls for hire.

Lucas sat up and planned the rest of the day. Eat two fried pork roll sandwiches and pork Valerie. See what more info he could collect on DG and get what he had to Warren. Try and get a little quality time looking at Herbert Banks. Maybe talk to Cat.

Rook called Valerie while he was frying up his sandwiches. The gods must have been paying him back for all his good works, because Valerie Moon had the day off, which meant a trip in from Fort Lee. Like the last time they met in the city, they went over to Nine West, where Tiffany was as gracious in packing up a pair of beige boots that weren't paid for as she was happy that she no longer had a cock.

"So nice to see you again," Tiffany said. "I'm sorry about the mix-up," which covered up that the register receipt showed zero.

"I don't know how you do that," said Valerie when they got outside. "It's like she owed you her life or something."

"Something like that."

"How about we grab some lunch before we grab each other?" said Valerie Moon. "A good steak, a cold beer."

"I could do that," Rook told her. He flagged the second cab that stopped for them and went over to Arthur's, where his gold shield counted as a reservation for two. They had New York strip, baked potatoes, and a couple of beers. Apple pie with vanilla ice cream and two spoons.

"You want to take me back to your office and interrogate me?" she asked on their way out.

"Have you been a bad girl?"

"I'm afraid I have, Detective."

When they got to his office she took off her sweater and tried on her new boots.

"You like?"

"I like," he told her.

Valerie Moon came over to him. "Are you shy, Detective?"

"I'm kind of all cut up, Val," he told her.

"Let me see," she said. "I'll make it all better."

"I'm not so sure."

"I am."

She took his shoes and socks off and then his pants. "I'll do all the work," she said.

Valerie was gentle, first with her hand, then her mouth, then riding him until they came together.

"I pronounce you're cured," she said. "I was worried about you."

"I'm okay," he said.

"I can see that, I mean I feel it. Your 'okay' is still running down my leg. You want to…"

"I'm good," he said. "You?"

"I meant show me where you had your operation."

"You want to see where I got shot and they cut me open?"

"Only if you want to show me."

"I'm good, Val."

The phone rang. It was Detective Antopol.

"I got to come over," he said.

28

Lucas got that look on his face that told Valerie it was time to go. She winked on her way out. "I know there's more where that came from," she said. "Call me."

Antopol was at the door in ten minutes. "First, I really need you to get me paid," Stanley said. "I'm getting squeezed big time."

"I told you I would," said Lucas.

Antopol lit up. "Right, right. But I need it yesterday. My ex is killing me. My lawyer says that under this case called *O'brien*, she can argue I got what they called 'enhanced earning capacity' even though the side work I'm doing's only temporary." He took a double hit of nicotine. "Christ, I'm already paying 25 percent support under the CSSA."

"That's bullshit," Lucas told him.

"That's not the half of it. She got the right to add in anything that 'offers personal economic benefit,' which is how she's asking for the records on my vehicle and then she's going to depose me about mileage and meals and whatnot." He finished his smoke. "I'm fucked."

"I get paid, you get paid. You need cash, it takes an extra day," Lucas told him. "The day's not over yet."

Antopol lit another Marlboro. "Look, I'm not trying to jam you up here, Rook. Let's try it this way. I'm still checking things out. I'm looking at some other couple of jackpots the dearly departed, Mr. Graves, has gotten his black ass into."

"Graves working those jobs with who?"

"He's partnered up with Herbie Banks. IAB takes a look, gives it a wink or whatever, Banko takes his pension and his stash and he's gone. DG partners up with Hy Gromek afterwards."

"Etillio's name show up?"

"Just rumors. And nobody else's."

"And who's making all this drama disappear, Detective Antopol?"

"Thought you'd get a kick out of this. Why it's then *Detective* Jaluski's running the job for Internal Affairs that goes nowhere."

Lucas rubbed out a pain that came up in his chest.

"You think he deep-sixed it for what?"

"Don't know that he did, Rook. Could be he couldn't come up with what he needed. Dwight was slick. Or somebody up the line sends it to the circular file because DG's a poster boy that he's colored and got his gold shield."

"Helluva job, Detective."

"Detective's right," said Antopol. "I detect that Jaluski gets wind of what I'm doing, I'm fucked royally. I'm fucked, Lucas Rook, and no way it's not behind working this thing for you. You're going to get the big money behind your getting shot up on this roof. Me, I'm going to be eating dog food and getting ass fucked from running this job for you."

"So you're asking me for some kind of kicker here, right, Stanley?"

"Another grand, Rook. You owe me that for what I got for you now. Which is who had his rat fuck eyes on Dwight Graves way back when, which didn't go nowhere, was no other than the fuck-face cheese-eating Frank Jaluski. That maybe helps you big-time some way, but it for sure puts me in the shitter."

"No way you're squeezing me. Only two people know you're working this little side job on Dwight is you and me," said Lucas. "And neither of us got anything to say. Your partner know anything about this?"

"Joey? Shit, no. Besides, he minds his own business."

"I'll get you a couple of hundred extra, Stan, but you think I'm doing more here, you got me confused with somebody else. You hear me?"

"Five, Rook."

"What I said. Don't push it."

"Right," said Antopol. "But you see where I'm coming from."

"I see we're done here. You did good detective work. You'll get paid. The rest is bullshit. The world's full of it."

"I get what you owe me and two fifty before the day's out," said Antopol and he left.

Lucas waited with his .45 to make sure Antopol didn't come back with some crazy idea in his head. You got crazy going, you see shit you got to clean up whether it's there or not.

So maybe Frank Jaluski's more than a jerkwad, cheese-eating rat fuck who's made it to lieutenant off of ruining other cops' lives. What was for sure was another trip to Florida to squeeze the truth out of Herbie Banks, who was now going to be getting his lying face introduced to a couple of his snow-globe things.

Lucas knew Banks was not going to be a pushover, and you're not a hundred percent yet means you don't go alone. Having some-body who would have your back was getting harder to find. Some of his old cop friends didn't want to chance running out their time without a hiccup. Some were already gone fishing. In the old days there was McCullagh and Tuze. Jimmy was living on the water somewhere. Ray Tuzio was in the ground. Lucas called Wingy Rosenzweig about the Glacas brothers.

"Just one day, Wingy. Out of town, Tampa. A one-day trip."

"Cost you a G and a half."

"Too much."

"Forget the half, my dear friend."

"You're a prince, Mr. Rosenzweig."

"Of course I am. And I'll book the travel, which you get at my cost. Getting you on the first flight back tomorrow's nothing.

Anybody asks when you check in tonight, you got a dying relative."

"Close enough, Wingy. Close enough."

Lucas Rook did his packing, which took about five minutes. You're going to beat the truth out of somebody, you don't need a fancy wardrobe.

29

That Wingy Rosenzweig got them booked on a flight to Tampa on short notice was no big deal. He had something going on with a Vicodin fan with access to frequent flyer miles. Vicodin man must have had a particularly insistent jones, because this time the tickets were first class, for which Wingy had said nothing about charging extra.

Lucas sipped his Jack Daniels. "How many marshals you make?" he asked Phil Glacas.

"One at 5B. There's supposed to be two, but maybe I'm missing somebody."

"Didn't think you did that."

"It happens, but either it doesn't matter or I have enough time to zero it out." He called the steward over for a ginger ale.

"You want to fill me in, Mr. Rook, that's fine. Mr. Rosenzweig told me you're meeting with a civilian, retired LEO."

"Correct. His law enforcement history got some old stink on him, which I'm not sure he wants to chat about. And I'm not all the way back from getting my chest split. The guy's named Herbert Banks. Used to be a detective back in the city before he became an asshole. Now he does super work at some apartment complex which I think he probably got a piece of." Rook finished his drink. "Anyways, he used to be a tough guy. Now he's an old tough guy. With the holes in me, I figured we're not quite even."

Glacas started his next question, but stopped as his soda arrived. Rook ordered another Jack.

"My parameters?"

"Nothing unless he gets frisky and I can't handle it," said Lucas. "If it goes that way, don't do anything that'll get us noticed."

"I'll make sure he's a good boy. It gets more than that, I'll handle it and I'm a ghost."

"Good, good." Lucas took a sip of whiskey and stretched his leg.

Glacas and Rook had their business to do with the airlines when they landed, which meant picking up the artillery that he had brought down. Nowadays, permitted or not, something like that could take a couple of hours depending on who had what bug up his ass, but the ghost man flashed something that got a nod from TSA and they were on their way packing.

There was a black SUV reserved at the car rental.

"Let's mount up," said Lucas like it was the good old days.

And off they went to hassle Dolly and Herbie and their dozens of snow globes and hundreds of kitties and probably thousands of Thomas Jeffersons.

Rook found Banko starting up his truck over at Perr's Real Estate. Glacas stayed three vehicles back, which was not an easy thing to do, and held the tail over to the Wildflower Condos. They waited for Banks to unload a vanity and his tools. They were in the service elevator with him. Lucas pushed the emergency stop button once the car started up.

Banks reached into his tool bag.

"Your hand went in, it stays in," said Glacas, showing his MP5.

"Christ, Rook, I thought it was a stick-up, for Christ sakes. You finally decide to put your ass down here?"

"Something like that, Banko. First I'm just driving around. Driving around. Then my realtor here, the gentleman with the heavy artillery, tells me I got to ask some questions. Do some re-search."

Banks started to pull up his hand.

"Don't," said the ghostman.

"Fuck you both," said Banks. "We had this before, Rook. I'm taking my inhaler out of my bucket here. You don't like it, do whatever. I'm not having no asthma attack for you or Dracula over there." He took out his Albuterol and used it.

"You getting allergies from counting all them old fifties, Herbie?" said Lucas.

He tipped the tool bucket over and sat down on it. "I got all day," he said. "So here we go, Banko. I ask, you answer. You fuck with me, my friend turns out your lights and then he does Dolly."

"That's doing her and me a favor," said Banks. "You want an update, I got none. You want a conversation, I'm not giving one. You want dispensation or whatever the fuck for what your brother did or did not do, I don't do that."

Lucas showed his Glock. "Etillio?"

"Never heard of him."

"I want Graves."

"My nigger partner? He was both. So that's all you get."

"What about Jaluski?"

"You want me to say I never heard of him. He was a family man? A cheese-eating fuck?" He took another puff of Albuterol.

"I get it you and him had an arrangement. You, him, and DG."

"And Etillio, your brother, Mayor Koch, fucking Johnny Carson. You're nuts and we're done here," said Banks.

Rook picked up the tools off the floor. "I guess we are. Sorry about the mess."

He pressed the button to open the door and broke Harry Banks' nose with a socket wrench.

"That's just because, Banko. Now you better see somebody, you look pretty fucked up."

Lucas called Rosenzweig about an earlier flight back from the bullshit visit that he had just made for what the Christ reason other than rearranging Herbie's face, which maybe was reason enough. Wingy came up with single seats, one in an hour and another two hours after, but Glacas wouldn't do it.

"My responsibility is until you're in your apartment, Mr. Rook."

"I appreciate that," said Rook. "We got the heavy lifting done. You have a beer."

"One light. My brother says two, but one it is."

"One light beer," Lucas said. "Three hundred ounces."

Phil didn't smile.

Rook found a decent seafood joint called the Shrimp Boat on the long way to the Tampa Airport. You're not riding with somebody half your age, you're talking about the song, *"Shrimp boats are a-coming..."* Then Patti Paige, *"How much is that doggie in the window?"* or her pussy. Nobody knows all that good shit anymore. Tuze, he's gone with his Aviator sunglasses with him. Ray thought Peggy Lee was an angel. Maybe she was, and with a little luck he's got his hand on her tit right now.

Lucas ate and drank like he meant it. Glacas did it like he was guarding the President. Then they rolled out to the airport to return the rental and check their hardware in.

The flight back to New York was quick and quiet, compliments of a Percocet and the bourbon chaser. As he swallowed the pill, Lucas decided that it would be his last one. They were addictive as hell, even if he had just delivered a beating. He stretched out his bad leg and thought about that little visit in the Florida sunshine, which told him if he ever did meet with Cholly the shrink, the diagnosis would be he was a knucklehead.

Hooray for America. Mexicans were working security at La Guardia, which meant they got jammed up over their weapons. Rook asked for and got a supervisor, who also was Mexican, only fatter and a female. The way up the ladder was clear.

Cops know how to wait, and the ghost was on the clock. Rook read the paper and Glacas read the crowd for an hour and a half until everything cleared.

"My brother's here to pick us up," Glacas said.

"I could grab a taxi or whatever," said Lucas.

"We'll complete the assignment," Phil told him.

They made the run back into the city and Glacas rode up on the elevator at the St. Claire.

"Mission accomplished," Rook told him as he tried to hand him some twenties.

"We're not permitted to accept gratuities. If you are pleased with our service, please convey that to Mr. Rosenzweig."

The ghost man rode downstairs after checking out Rook's apartment. Lucas kicked off his shoes and checked the messages on his machine. A couple of calls from Gracey that she was alright, which meant she wasn't. A reminder about the lawyer's meeting. And Owls just leaving his name.

Rook was about to hit the shower when Catherine Wren called.

"Father needs to move closer to me. We looked at a couple of places, but he is reluctant," she said.

"I hear that. He leaves the city, he thinks he stops doing whatever keeps him alive."

"Something like that. I had a reservation for us at seven at Longden's but I didn't hear from you."

"Sorry, Catherine, I was working. How about I order in Chinese? We watch a movie with subtitles, drink some wine."

"Perfect, Lucas, I'll see you at eight," she said. "If Father takes some more settling down and I'll be later, I'll call."

Lucas unplugged the phone and stretched out on the sofa. A lot more of that since he got shot, but shit, cops look forward to extra sleep like a teenager does a blow-job in the back of his parents' car. Maybe the only good thing to come out of what happened on the roof was when the crazy dreams came, and they always did, hello Ray Tuzio and a world of snow globes, he was really too tired to give a shit. Cholly would tell him that's progress, healing, whatever the fuck that meant. Healing's when the holes in you or your twin brother were never there.

He was out for an hour and a half. A knock on the door. He hadn't ordered the chink food yet. Maybe Catherine coming early. Just as likely somebody coming to fuck with him about something, the apartment, the grand jury tomorrow.

He answered the door with his .45 behind his back.

"Did I wake you up?" said Grace Savoy.

"How could you tell?"

"I'm sorry," she said. "I thought I might take you out for a drink, to apologize for being such a ninny. That's one of my favorite words, 'ninny.' And I could tell the way you walked over to the door, plus I could hear you sleep breathing."

She came in.

"It smells like you were sleeping."

"How's that, Grace?"

"Kind of toasty, manly. That sounded nice, man on toast."

"I'm going out, Grace."

"Business?"

"Catherine."

"We could all go out. Double date."

Lucas went in to get a cold beer.

"And who would that be with, neighbor? Or shouldn't I ask."

Grace lit a cigarette. "Oh, me you, Catherine, The Swan. He's so elegant."

"I'm tired, Gracey. Tomorrow's going to be a long day."

"Sorry. I'll see you tomorrow morning. Can we ride in together or something?"

"I'll check on you when I get back tonight, Gracey."

"That would be nice. Please do that." She leaned in and kissed him on the forehead. "No matter how late you get home."

Right, like checking the doors in the good old days walking the beat. At least then Kirk wasn't dead and dirty or both and he hadn't taken those slugs and then had his chest cut open. So maybe they were the good old days.

Lucas went over and plugged his phone back in. Catherine calling to say Daddy did just fine and can she meet him at The Brothers at 8:30. Time enough for a shower. Casual clothes, good burgers, maybe she stays over.

He put on the black turtleneck and the sports jacket he got from Muskrat, which fit a little big since he hadn't been working out. No shoulder rig yet. He wore the little Glock pancake style and went out into the street.

Rook got to The Brothers only five minutes late, which meant five minutes early cop time. Catherine came wearing her New York clothes.

"Am I overdressed?" she asked. "The pearls?"

"You're fine, Cat. You look just fine."

She leaned in and kissed him. "You have some spots on your shoe," she said.

"Paint."

"You're lying to me. I can tell by your face. It's blood, isn't it? I can tell. You told me…"

"You're wrong, Cat. Let's sit down." Lucas took her by the arm. "You've got a lot going on, your father…"

"I can't lose you," she said. "It's too much with my father. You getting into fights, getting shot. You said you'd talk to somebody about it."

"I called for an appointment."

"I need you, Lucas Rook."

He took out his cell and dialed Dr. Hepburn. Cholly answered the call on the first ring.

"Rook, I got caller ID. I'm about to start a session."

"I need an appointment."

"Real or pretend?"

"Real."

"Okay, six p.m. Friday. They're all real and pretend."

"Six p.m. Friday," Lucas repeated for Catherine's benefit.

"And two other things, I don't take insurance."

"You don't take insurance."

"And I may be wearing my jammies."

"Swell, Doctor. I'll see you then."

"Thank you," she said.

"No problem, Cat. Come on back to my place. We can get into our PJ's and order in."

30

Schwarzman's office called that they wanted to send a car for him, but Lucas knew he would be paying for it one way or another and maybe with some kind of add-on if the judge billed like Warren Phelps did. Besides, he had things to do on the way. Things meant ham and eggs at Joe Oren's and a shine on his black shoes.

Joe and Sam were both out front, Oren working the register and the cook handling the counter. A new girl, a thin blonde, was waiting the tables. She offered a firm handshake as Lucas sat down.

"I'm a friend of Jeanie's. She told me to call you 'Uncle Lucas' and that she has first dibs." She poured him a cup of coffee.

Sam went to the window into the kitchen and brought out two fried eggs, an order of ham, and a side of rye toast. He picked at a piece of eggshell on the plate.

"Trying to get my nephew growing up right. Saw you come in the door, Lucas Rook. No need to keep you waiting, especially you got your suit on, which means wedding or funeral."

"Gracey's court day today. I read it in the paper," said Joe.

"Don't read no papers 'til my day's over. Read them on the train uptown and see what kind of life my horoscope's been," said Sam.

"I hear that," said Lucas. "How's Jeanie?"

"She's good," said her father. "Got an interview today at some fancy salon. Good to get her away from this joint."

Lucas drank half his coffee and started on the breakfast.

"She's finishing up school though," Sam said as he turned back into the kitchen. "You don't finish what you started, it comes back and finishes you down the road. You feel me, nephew?"

"Truer words were never spoken," said Rook. "That boyfriend of hers behaving, Joe?"

"No problems," said Joe. "Which is the best I can ask for."

"You want me to check on the salon place?" Rook asked.

"Couldn't hurt. I'll get you the exact name. Your leg bothering you again? I got some arnica in my office."

"Good to go, Joseph," said Lucas. "The Swan says bring my cane with me, I bring it." He went over to the counter. "Your nephew did alright, Samuel. I'll be back."

The cook leaned across the counter. "I'm not telling him a word. Let him get to know about that hot grill plenty before he hears a word."

Not that his bad leg wasn't for shit. It would never be right, but you're walking with a cane, you're inviting the gangbangers and the muggers to take a bite, and until he was back to being able to pull-put the wolves' teeth, there's no reason to invite trouble. He went out into the street carrying the cane like he had no actual need for it, then went back into Oren's.

"How about a tomato sandwich, Sam."

"Going to see the shineman? I'll make that myself. Sometimes the simplest thing can get a beginner cook's head just spinning."

Sam was back out in five minutes with a paper bag. "Made your friend two," he said.

"Appreciate it," said Lucas and he went on to see Jimbo Turner.

The shineman was up on his stand when Rook got there.

"How you doing?" Lucas asked him.

"Not bad for a diabetic, old white shineman. Except the chiropodist, podiatrist, they call themselves now, told me to not to be on my feet so much. I says sure. I'll stand on my hands and do my work. Now let me get on down and you get on up. Seems I want to do a fine job and earn them tomato sandwiches you got there in that bag."

Lucas climbed into the chair. "Your smeller's working just fine, Jimbo. Sam made these from over Joe Oren's for you."

"Will you thank both them gentlemen for me and not say that they're not wrapped up good. I can smell what you're carrying. My lamps get dimmer, the rest of my senses just get better, and it don't matter whether they say that's an old wives' tale or not."

He started in on Rook's shoes. First the wash, then a coat of black he rubbed in with his finger, the brushes clickety-clack, clickety-clack.

"You going someplace special, Mr. Rook, we going to put some cream on them." The brushes again and the rag, snapping and popping while he made it work. Then a drop of peppermint oil and last, the piece of nylon stocking he kept in the drawer underneath the chair. Jimbo Turner put another drop of peppermint on his old hands and rubbed them together a couple of times.

"Wished I could get this oil in them Duane Reede's or whatever. I get them drug companies or whatever to listen to me, I'm retired a long, long time ago."

He offered Rook his shoulder to get down and used the whisk broom on Rook's jacket, front and back. Lucas paid him and handed over the bag. Doing otherwise, you're not giving him the respect for what he does.

The Swan's office was like one of those gentleman's clubs. Thick carpet, dark furniture. Enough to tell you that your money was going to be well spent.

The receptionist was an older woman with a serious attitude. "Judge Schwarzman is expecting you," she said. "Conference Room B, second door on the right."

The Swan came in. He had his going to court outfit on. Pin-striped suit, white shirt, two-million-dollar necktie.

"I got the subpoena," said Rook.

Schwarzman sat at the head of the long mahogany table.

"We shall see what we shall see."

"I'm not very happy with surprises, Counselor. Fill me in."

"A lot of paper's flying around, which I can either tell you about or show you copies. Some has been filed on Ms. Savoy's behalf by Warren. We have begun suit for your injuries…"

"Not against the PD. I was clear about that."

"Of course," said Schwarzman. "Mr. Phelps has filed against the Police Department, the City, the St. Claire, and against Mr. Graves' estate."

Lucas rolled his neck. "Don't tell me we have no action from Felix Gavilan?"

"Very aggressive fellow," said The Swan. "But I don't think he'll get very far here."

"And this has what to do with the preliminary hearing this morning?"

"Maybe everything. Maybe nothing," answered Schwarzman.

"Meaning what?"

"What the DA does is up to them. My own surmise, although it is just that, is that they know everything about all the civil litigation. They will see me sitting with you. And then they will become reasonable."

"About what?"

"About everything," said Schwarzman.

"These word games is why cops hate lawyers," said Lucas.

"That's what we do, Mr. Rook. Specifically, what is going to happen is we're going to take a ride down to Centre Street so you can meet with Art Cooper."

"Who is?"

"The latest ADA assigned to this case, another step up the ladder from Vechione. Now to this morning." He poured himself a glass of water. "As I mentioned before and as you well know, you are the prosecution's witness, so of course you tell the truth."

"About what?"

"You were on the roof. You saw her shoot the detective. That's all they want now."

"But they can also get what they don't want, Counselor."

Schwarzman picked up his briefcase. "Cooper's good at his job. He'll ask you very narrow questions to exclude everything else he doesn't want in. They only have to show a prima facie case."

"But he sees me with you now, he knows I'm going to help the City get killed in the civil case."

"Precisely. So maybe they don't want to crucify a blind girl whose friend, you, knows that Dwight Graves had it coming to him."

"And you're going to see they get crucified in our suit for damages," said Lucas.

"Correct," said Schwarzman. "Now give me a minute or so to primp. Then we can take a ride and help your friend, Ms. Savoy."

"Sounds like a plan, Judge," said Rook. "A very clever one."

31

Rook had been in a courtroom a hundred times when he was at the PD. Whether it was a particularly evil motherfucker going to get it, or whether a scummer's lawyer was going to try to tie Rook's balls in a knot, it was always halfway alright, because you got paid for court time. You wanted the extra cash when you were in uniform, you would go crazy making arrests, turnstile jumpers, squeegy men. After he got his gold shield, there could be all the OT you needed.

You always knew what you were going to say before you got sworn. You had been prepped by the DA, which sometimes could be pretty lame. And the older guys on the job would run you through it until you knew the game yourself. The general rules always were if you can answer 'yes' or 'no,' you do that. You don't anticipate where the lawyer is trying to take you because he may know something you don't. Also, it's okay to say 'I don't remember.' And it's okay to lie.

Schwarzman's car dropped them off early at the court on Centre Street so anything that was going to happen before the preliminary could happen.

When they got upstairs, there was lots of drama going on. Fast lawyers talking to their clients, who were trying to get used to their suits. A half-dozen cops standing around waiting to be called. An old-timer gave Rook the high sign.

"Mr. Cooper would like to talk to me," said The Swan. "And I'm always willing to listen. I'll see you inside."

Felix Gavilan's "secretary" was already in the courtroom sitting next to a big colored lady who must have been the dead prick Dwight Graves' relative. Grace came in. She looked terrible, pale, shaking, and walking like she was blind, which she never did. It was going to be a regular freak show, which should have never happened except that the pus bag who Gracey shot was a cop and on top of that, he was a black cop.

The professional civic rights fucks were there, half of them being paid by somebody with another agenda, the old leftist Anti-War, now the pro gay marriage, pro abortion anarchist fucks. The other half because it got them free press for their churches or whatever so they could make a buck later.

They all waited for the circus to start, the paid lawyers in their fancy clothes, the public defenders in their righteousness. The troublemakers. The cops watching the meter tick. Grace was getting agitated.

"Are you here, neighbor man? I can tell you're here." She changed her accent. "Help me," she said.

Judge Russell was on the bench, which meant no bullshit. "I'll clear this courtroom."

Somebody yelled something which got them taken out.

"Anybody else looking for a contempt citation, I will oblige," said the judge. "Call the next case," he told the clerk.

Enrique patted the Graves lady's big hand. Judge Russell heard a smash and grab, which he held over and then called a brief recess.

Lucas went out into the hall. No Schwarzman, no Warren Phelps, no greasy Gavilan. He went back inside and over to the clerk, a thick white guy with a red face.

"Breen, right?"

"Rook, how you been? Heard you got shot, which I guess you're here for that case."

"Cooper around?"

"I ain't seen him. Let me go find out what's up, which'll give me an opportunity to take my twentieth piss of the day. Saw palmetto my ass."

"Coop is in a pow-wow, so something's going on," the clerk said when he got back. "I'll try and find out if they're moving your thing to the afternoon or what."

The next case went on until the lunch break. Lucas caught Breen as he was getting to go to lunch.

"What's up, Breenie?"

"For me it's my wife's tortellini and sausage and then maybe a snooze. His Honor enjoys his extended periods of recreation. Competitive son of a gun."

"I got to hang around or what?"

The clerk looked at the list. "I wouldn't, but then they didn't subpoena me. You're going to ask me about Coop? I don't know nothing except my last trip to the gents', I see some big nig from the City with a bunch of lawyers, The Swan, Phelps, some Latin guy."

"You're a prince, Breenie. If it was the old days, I'd get you some tickets for the Knicks."

"If it was the old days I'd want them tickets. Clyde, Willis, Dollar Bill. Where are they when we need them? Except Bradley thinks it's the '60s, he's with Osama Obama." He shook his brown paper bag. "Now if you'll excuse me, I'm going to eat some home cooking, read the paper, and so on."

"Appreciate it," said Lucas. "You tell me where the pow-wow's being held, I'll find out whether I got to hang around."

"Judge Wallenstein's chambers, who's on vacay. But I didn't tell you that."

Rook walked down the hall and around. Felix Gavilan and Warren Phelps were talking on their cells. Warren was headed to the men's room. More than a few important confabs happened in bathrooms, and you're talking about deals with lawyers, half of them belong there.

The Swan came out of Judge Wallenstein's.

"You're wanting to ask how we're faring, Lucas. Things are going well. You're wanting to ask if you'll get called today, I'd say maybe. If your presence is requested, I'll call you on your cell."

"Appreciate that, Judge."

Rook went down and out of the courthouse. He thought he saw the judge sliding out the side door with a paddle and goggles in his right hand.

There were a couple of decent watering holes in walking distance. The Docket was a place mostly lawyers went, which meant that was out on general principles. A block down was the Bored Room, which despite its corporate reference, got a lot of cops and had a menu that you felt like you had eaten something after you ate, meatloaf with mashed, chicken croquettes, sandwiches you didn't have to eat two of.

There was a spot at the bar next to Della Penna, who was deeply engrossed in the racing form, but looked up when he saw who was sitting down.

"How's it hanging, Rook?" he said. "You doin' alright?"

"I'm doing. How's by you, Lou?"

"Good, good. I got this all scoped out. 'Cupie's Girl' in the third."

"You think, Lou?"

"Sure, sure."

The bartender came over. "Roast pork's good," he said. "So's the meatball parm. What are you drinking?"

Lucas had the parm and two Miller Lites with *The Daily News* he grabbed from the booth behind him. No call from The Swan, but you sit around the saloon long enough, you're going to get loaded. He walked a couple of blocks north and then the long way back.

When Lucas checked the courtroom, the handball-playing Judge Russell was up on the bench. The defendant, who was Cambodian or Laotian, had better hope the match went good.

Rook walked around the hall to where the meeting was and then went back outside. Maybe the Bored Room had decent coffee and he could impress some of the patrons with his business cards with the chess piece on it. His phone rang.

"Back tomorrow, Lucas," said The Swan.

"I thought the prelim had to be completed in one day."

"Usually, but under 180.60 (10), it can be adjourned in the interest of justice. But in the absence of good cause, only for one day."

"We got that here, Counselor?"

"Justice or good cause?" asked Schwarzman. "Could be either or both. In any case, we've got a lot of work to do. I'm talking to the insurance company for the St. Claire tomorrow."

"Gracey doing alright?"

"Warren's being Warren, so she's fine. He's already objected to expert reports as hearsay and he's got it out there that we should be looking at misdemeanors. The stuff his PI dug up on Dwight Graves made Cooper's head spin. I'll call you later. In the meantime, I got my own magic to do."

Lucas Rook grabbed a taxi to his office. The driver was an old foreign guy trying to make small talk about the Jets so he'll get more than the tip you give to an illegal alien. Rook did Boris halfway right and then told him that Joe Namath wore panty hose, which the guy repeated as if it meant something to him.

Lucas finished up his paperwork on the Circuit City job. A little luck and they pay him quick without jerking him around on his billing.

Maybe Gracey got some good luck and he gets something for getting drilled up on that roof. Not that he believed in luck, unless it was bad or somebody else's. Sid Rosen, philosopher and auto mechanic, said both of them kinds of luck were karma, which is screwy crap that losers tell themselves when their lives get shit on.

32

You get shot or the sky falls on you, you still got bills to pay. Lucas put them in due date order and then took a look at his checking account and what was in the credit union. Time to divide the bills into three piles. The dentist could wait until hell freezes over, the office rent could wait another week, the payment for his liability insurance couldn't. At least there wasn't the medical insurance. He went out on disability from the beating Etillio and his boys gave him, so he got that for life. And the apartment rent, The Swan had told him to hold off on that to give them something to think about.

On the plus side was the disability payments from the City, which were another reason he wasn't going to sue the PD. Some money coming in from the Circuit City. The dollars from the peeper job in Jersey had come and gone. His slice from Owls Miksis for running down Graves was waiting on Warren Phelps' check clearing, which was supposed to be today.

Lucas was about to call over for a sausage and mushrooms when the phone rang. Fifty-fifty, you got some dothead pretending his name is Chuck and trying to sell you a combination of satellite television and a time share in the Poconos.

"My name is Daniel Tabb, I'm calling from our regional headquarters at Circuit City."

"Good to talk to you, Mr. Tabb." The sound of the register ringing.

"We appreciate your service, and I'd like to speak to you about something else."

"I'd like to listen," said Lucas.

"Your office in an hour, Mr. Rook? I'm on a rather tight schedule."

"They just painted it, Mr. Tabb. How about I meet you in front of the clock in the lobby of the Waldorf?" Which is a lot more conducive to anything than his one-room office, which even if it had a waiting room was a little iffy.

"That's just fine, Mr. Rook. Just fine."

Enough time to get back to the St. Claire to get all dolled up. Lucas took the third taxi that went by and changed into his Private Eye turtleneck and the fancy leather jacket he had bought from the Muskrat. Beautiful and well-informed, what more could Mr. Tabb ask for.

You're running a business, you make business decisions, like the landlord for 166th Fifth's going to get paid a week late. You're running a big business like Circuit City, you make big business decisions, like telling thousands of your employees they don't have their jobs anymore, but if they want to, they can reapply in a couple of weeks and you'll be happy to reward them by paying them less. One of your people accidentally finds a bunch of terrorists stupid enough to think they're going to blow up Fort Dix, you get tons of free pub so you're back not looking bad. Circuit City got enough to give you a crumb or two.

Gransback, the hotel's guy, was coming out of the St. Claire with two Japs as Rook went in. A lot of Asians are buying New York real estate, or maybe they're just after the laundry contract. "Looking forward to chatting, Mr. Rook," he said.

Lucas nodded and went up to his apartment. Since all that up on the roof and the cops around and whatever, he had ramped his security routine, which meant leaving two pieces of tape on the door, or a piece of plastic straw in the doorjamb to go with the new alarm system. He still left the bathroom door open, and now there was another mirror so he could check the place from the opposite direction. The .357 that used to be stashed in the hallway and wound up in Gracey's hands was in the DA's evidence locker. But there was the hardware he got from Leavitt in easy reach.

He took a quick shower and patted his incisions and the bullet holes dry. Doc DiBona would say he's "healed nicely," which made his still wearing the Kevlar vest perfectly nuts. But so was getting gut shot again or thumped in the chest by some hard case. Time to try the shoulder rig with the turtleneck, which would make any exec think he was the perfect man for the next job.

The way he had handled the in-store scams for Circuit City was perfecto, so maybe he'd get a monthly retainer to replace the one he had lined up with the funeral parlor empire before everything got sidetracked. Which reminded him, now that he's not looking half-dead, time to call on Hugh Sirlin and see if he could get something up and running again on that bone snatching.

The Waldorf lobby was busy as it always was. Lots of foreigners acting like they were all Princess Grace and her husband and shopping their asses off. A big man, maybe 6'5", 250 came over. Very pale skin, very strong handshake.

"I got us a table," he said. And they went into the bar area.

"I'm guessing you got my photo from when I was out at your stores."

"Correct." He had a red drink on the little table. "We also have a strict alcohol policy, which explains the cranberry and soda. You?"

"Iced tea is good."

"I guess you know what's going on. We've eliminated the positions of approximately thirty-four hundred employees. They each received a severance package and they're being invited to apply for the newly created positions at a compensation in the current market range. At the same time, we have the well-deserved appreciation of the public because of the fortuitous circumstances involving the near-tragedy at Fort Dix, New Jersey."

"The labor thing must not have made too many people happy other than your shareholders."

"I appreciate you did your homework, Mr. Rook. Actually the shares rose almost two percent."

"How can I help you?" Rook asked him.

"We're considering outsourcing a number of functions, HR, security."

The iced tea came. "That's good business, Dan."

"We're number two in the marketplace and there's lot of competition."

"I'm interested in a monthly retainer. I don't need benefits."

Dan Tabb took a taste of his drink.

"I don't do numbers, Mr. Rook, just people. I'm a people person. I just wanted to tell you we're interested and get to know you a bit."

"I like baseball, I hate cats and I drink beer."

"I followed what happened in the papers. That must have been pretty rough, Mr. Rook. We're glad to see you're up and around."

"Which is why the meeting."

"That and to get my personal impression." Tabb looked at his watch.

"I'm up and around and interested," Rook said.

"I'm glad to hear that. In the meantime, are you interested in another short term assignment?"

Lucas sipped his tea. "I'm listening, Mr. Tabb."

"First Amendment rights, we respect them. As to disagreeing with our policies, that is. When it comes to blabbing about ways to rob us, that's a different matter."

Rook sipped his iced tea and wished it was a lager. "The gift card thing, receipt switch, swapping the merch, I've seen it all."

"I'm sure you have. The latest is they rent the items. Buy the camcorder or big screen, do the event, return the thing. We lose the profit on the sale, more often than not, we can't sell the unit as new, and we've got the restocking expenses." He looked at his watch again. "If I don't get to American Girl, I'm going to get massacred when I get home. The return scam, we're addressing with RFD tags, but right now, there's an expensive issue involving register tapes."

"It's like stealing the paper from the mint," Lucas said. "You can print your own currency on your laptop."

"Precisely. Our inventory control indicates we've got a loss at our Rego Park store. We'd like you to put an end to it, particularly because we think the perpetrator is the one publicizing the scams on the Internet. The manager's name is Mendez. He has all the particulars. We'd like you to get on this as soon as possible."

"I'll move some things around, Mr. Tabb. I like to keep my clients happy."

"Excellent, Mr. Rook. I'm sure it will go far in our evaluation of you for the permanent outsourced position. And now if you will excuse me, I've got to get to that doll place or I'm a dead man."

Lucas thought about asking if he needed backup, but you don't joke with tight-asses who control what you got. He went back downtown to get his Mercury for a run on the scenic Brooklyn Queens Expressway.

Rego Park had changed. It was no longer the haven for European immigrants trying to forget where they came from. It was all about the Benjamins, and not Sol and Molly Benjamin, but the natives rolling out hundred-dollar bills, coming into a Circuit City where you have a manager named Mendez.

Rook took his clipboard out of the Merc, put a pencil behind his ear and went into the store. The manager's wearing a clip-on tie and a name tag that says "Don."

"Please come in and close the door," he says.

Not too many Latin Donalds. Unless it's his title, *Don Diego Alejandro, Miguel Mendez* or some shit like that. They exchanged cards. Don was duly impressed with the chess piece on Rook's.

"You're familiar with our operation, Mr. Rook?" He offered a chair.

"I've done work for the company before."

"And you understand our problem."

"Register tape's going out the back door, then coming in the front."

Mendez got up. "Loss Prevention's part of it."

"Okay."

"The other part is who I think is behind it."

"And that is?"

The manager sat back down. "Sorry, all this stuff makes me kind of…"

Lucas arched his back. "What you tell me stays with me, Mr. Mendez. I work for you."

"I appreciate that. Between us, I'm reasonably sure I know who the person is."

"You have surveillance."

"Video, but I can't be sure it shows what…"

"I'll take a look. I'll take a look around. You want me to hold off interviewing until you get my opinion of your video?"

Mendez stood up again. "Exactly."

"And what special characteristics does our employee have?"

"Excuse me?"

"Something's got you agitated, Don."

Mendez took a deep breath. "I guess you're right. There's a couple of things. He's an older man, which means I have to be concerned about age discrimination claims. He's white. He used to be a union guy. We don't have unions here. But with the lay-offs we just put in place, we don't want trouble with any labor groups or whatever."

"That makes good sense, Don. Except for one thing."

An uh-oh look on the manager's face.

"What's wrong, Mr. Rook?"

"You said 'a couple of things.' You gave me three. Anything else?"

Mendez thought about it for a minute and then smiled. "Not that I can think of," he said. "Let me give you what I have." He unlocked the bottom drawer of his metal desk and handed over the tapes.

"I think I should watch these alone," Lucas told him. "So my decision-making is unbiased."

"Of course, of course. I understand, Mr. Rook." And the less I have to do with this, the better.

Rook looked at the surveillance. No doubt the suspect was the doer, but there could always be more than one. He pretended to watch the surveillance a couple of more times through and made some notes so that he'd have some decent billing. When he went out on the floor, Don was arguing with a freckle-faced lady. "I'm sorry, Miss, we do not negotiate the prices lower than they are already marked."

"Well then, you can lay this big screen TV off this cart the way you lay off your workers."

Mendez excused himself and came over to Rook.

"Do you have what you need?"

"Not quite," said Lucas. "Another time would nail it. I'll call you when I get back to my office to set up another appointment."

The other time at the store would be pure bullshit. A blind man, Grace Savoy, could see what was going on.

Lucas was just getting onto the Expressway when his phone rang. It was her. You think about somebody, they call, Sid Rosen says that's "synchronicity," whatever that means.

"Twenty-six thousand fifty-one," she said.

"Again, Gracey."

"Two, six zero, point, five, one," she told him. "That's good, right? Warren says that's very good."

"260.51 of the New York Penal Code is very good if that's what you're talking about. Criminal possession of a weapon in the fourth degree. That's just a misdemeanor, Gracey."

"Plus they're going to let me work, which means we both get paid, and Warren says they'll let me go even if it's out-of-state because I've got us a shoot and it's just in Philadelphia and we'll not be gone overnight."

"Phelps is the king," Lucas said.

"And so are you and so is The Swan. Christ, I need to be pretty again," said Grace Savoy and she hung up.

33

Most of the big deal about Jackie Robinson breaking the color line was bullshit. Another one went in a couple of days later and nobody even knows his name. What wasn't bullshit was Chock Full o' Nuts, which Robinson was vice president of. You could get a damned good cup of coffee anytime at any of them, but like most of the spots that weren't for shit, they closed down.

Lucas was coming out of the elevator on his way to try a new coffee joint that had just opened up two blocks away, "Joe's Joe," which was probably owned by some French-Saudi conglomerate, when a well-dressed man with a large briefcase came up to him.

"My name is Harold Edelman."

"What are you selling?" Rook asked.

"I'm the occupational and physical therapist ordered by Dr. DiBona."

"Have a nice day, Hal."

"Dr. DiBona sent me," he said.

"Can we do this across the cup of coffee I'm about to have? Otherwise you've got no shot. With all due respect to the good doctor."

Edelman nodded and Lucas took him over to the new place.

"This isn't going to work," Rook said when they got there.

"I'm a certified occupational therapist and licensed physical therapist, Mr. Rook. And I have reviewed your chart thoroughly with Dr. DiBona, who..."

213

"I meant this place. It's just another crapachino joint in disguise."

"I have the time blocked out, Mr. Rook."

"He sends you a lot of patients, does he?" Lucas asked. "Well, you got to eat, too. You can do what you got to do if you can do it now, but I'm not putting my hand in my pocket to spend six bucks for a cup of coffee."

"Deal," said the therapist and they sat down.

"We have no servers," called the serious caffeine technician from behind the counter.

"Black, no whipped cream, froth, nutmeg or whatever," said Rook.

"I hear you," said Edelman and he went over and placed their order.

"My tea has to steep over there," he said when he came back, "but we can get started. The medical records provided to me, and such were completely HIPAA compliant, indicate limitations on your activities of daily living, functional tasks and those job related."

"I'm fine, Mr. Therapist, but knock yourself out."

A bell rang, which meant their order was ready. Edelman ignored it. The bell rang again. Edelman ignored it.

"Now we're talking," said Lucas. "Go on."

"Your PMH, past medical history, is significant for right orbital fracture…"

"Lucky punch."

"GSW x 2. Multiple bilateral fractures to the lower extremities."

"Dancing with the Stars," said Lucas.

The bell rang again.

"I better get that, Mr. Rook."

He came back with his red zinger and Rook's coffee.

"We need to secure a functional analysis, including mobility, ADL, homemaking, and the like…"

"Homemaking?"

"That's a term of art, you know, cooking, cleaning and the like. Also I need to secure a job analysis." He tried a little smile. "Then I will design a treatment plan consistent with your occupational and kinetic goals."

"My kinetic goals and my homemaking," said Lucas.

Edelman picked up his cup of tea, then put it down. "I'm just trying to do my job, Mr. Rook, and the therapy will do you good. Your gait is poor, if you don't mind me telling you. And your guarding needs to be addressed, not to mention getting where you can exercise again. The asymmetry is noticeable."

"Like hitting the bag?"

"You'll have to work up to that, but sure. And I could do wonders with that leg of yours."

"So this would actually do me good. Right, Hal?"

"Absolutely."

"You got a female therapist? Eurasian, big tits?"

"I'll look into that, Mr. Rook."

"And I'll keep that appointment."

Edelman raised his cup. "Deal," he said.

"No way I'm drinking coffee that's six bucks a pop no matter who's paying. You sit and enjoy yourself. Write this all up, whatever. I'm rolling."

Lucas walked over another block and got himself a couple of Sabrette's with the works and a cold bottle of Stackie's root beer that really hit the spot.

Then Rook went back to his place. The therapy would be good if it at least got him banging the heavy bag. The best he could do right now was some shadow boxing which his grandmother could handle. That, get back on the bench, he wouldn't have to be wearing that Kevlar vest for any bullshit job like for Gracey.

Gransback had slipped a note of apology under Rook's door about "permitting someone in the lobby without properly screening their solicitation intentions." The last time anybody solicited him at all was the last time he was down on The Stroll, looking for info on that rat Westie who used to be Red Maguire. As penance "The St. Claire Family" would be presenting him a month of the *Sunday New York Times*, which they hoped he would enjoy. Other than the sports, he should run out and buy a parrot or whatever so he'd have some use for that liberal rag.

Rook started the tub and put his handgun in the soap dish. Catherine always loved that gesture of humanity. He took a Pepcid, because of the hot dogs, and soaked. "The St. Claire Family" should be giving him a tub with a whirlpool, which he would talk to Schwarzman about.

The phone rang. Then stopped, then started again, either another oversees jitbag marketer pretending his name was "Jack" instead of Mahatma, or something important. Most likely it was something in-between, which is what it was, when he picked up the third call.

"Hello, dearie," said Grace. "The fashion shoot I've had on hold until I found out I wasn't going to get the chair, it's tonight."

"That's nice of you, Gracey. Particularly since you hadn't given me any of the details to begin with other than it was in Philly. Not to mention how it's come up so fast."

"Excuse me," she said. "I was too busy getting freed from the gallows. In any case, it is apparently cheaper to embrace a faux Rocky statue in a Bronx warehouse than the real thing in front of the Philadelphia Art Museum. I'll be by at five, honey, since the travel's out. You can plow me if you want to."

"We've got a job to do, Gracey. You being beautiful. Me being imposing and ill-tempered, if necessary."

"Okay then," she said. "Bring one of your big guns. I don't like the Bronx, not one bit."

"Sure, Grace. Everything will be fine. I'll see you soon."

The shoot did not go well, not that the Bronx location posed any threat. First, the driver doesn't show, not that you could blame him. A big difference in what they're paying you to go down to Philly, hang around for five, six hours, take the Turnpike back Instead you drop us off at Inwood Avenue, we call you come on back. Your time is shot. You get paid shit.

Gracey wanted a limo. Larry and his fancy cravat would only pay so much for local expenses, which would not cover the premium any of the limousine services were happy to gouge you with on such short notice. The limo that Sid had was in use for some historic after-prom party.

Then Grace was not going to go at all until Lucas was able to convince her that Sid's caddy was "romantic." Then there was the battle of whether she could smoke in the car, which she insisted on and Rosen absolutely refused. "You get that smell in, you cannot get it out," he said. "Unless you use a commercial odor remover and then you can't get the smell of that out."

They drove the Caddy back into the garage and Lucas pulled the Avanti out.

"Get in," he told her.

"What is this?"

"It's mine. Duck your head."

"I feel like I'm being 'taken for a ride.' "

"Could be." He revved the engine.

"That's nice," she said. "The sound. Kind of growly. Can I smoke?" she said. "I have to smoke before I work."

"Knock yourself out, Gracey."

They went up to the Bronx to a factory that made perfume packaging. You're shooting an ad for perfume, that makes sense. The lights were hot. The crew was non-union. The boxing trunks for Gracey were too big. Her nipples wouldn't stand up, despite the fact they rubbed ice cubes across them.

Little Lawrence was smoking one French cigarette after another, which made Gracey want to smoke. They took a couple of breaks for that and tried turning on the air-conditioning to help with Gracey's nipples.

"I'll make them get hard," said one of the lighting techs.

"You can do mine while you're at it," said another.

"Everyone just shut up," said Larry.

"You could suck on them," Gracey said. "That always seems to work."

"You too, Ms. Savoy. Go do whatever you have to do. Ten minutes, then we're back at it. I cannot afford to run over budget," said Lawrence.

"You also cannot afford to do more than look at these nipples," said Gracey.

"Do whatever, Ms. Savoy, to get those nipples erect. Whatever turns you on. Shoot somebody if you have to. That's seemed to work in the past. Maybe Mr. Bodyguard over there can lend you his Gat. Ten minutes, not twelve. And no crying, none whatsoever. It makes your eyes look like you're having some kind of allergic attack."

That got Grace sulking, which got Lawrence yelling again.

Lucas came over. "You alright?"

"I cannot work like this," she said, which she did not mean. "He said I should go shoot somebody like I did on our patio and then maybe my nipples would stand up."

"He what?"

She repeated what her Lawrence had said, word for word.

Rook walked in at little Larry.

"Get away from me. Do not touch me. What do you think this is? First, you're off my set. Second, take her with you. Third, you'll be hearing from my lawyer."

"No, Larry, don't. Everything's just fine now," she said.

Lucas stopped, but gave it one of his best menacing poses.

"It is not fine. Shut it down, I'll get what's-her-name back," said the producer.

"There is no other me," said Grace.

"Thank God," said the producer. "Manhattan would be littered with dead bodies and blind girls tripping over them."

Grace slapped him. The crew applauded.

"This shoot is cancelled, Ms. Savoy. And so is your contract."

"You work for me, Lawrence. And you are a little shit, but do reschedule and I will see if my agency will allow me to give you a second chance."

"What about us?" said one of the light men.

"You're all wonderful and you'll be paid, of course," said Grace. She turned to Lucas. "Can we stop for a milkshake on the way home?"

"Sure we can," said Rook. "Sure we can."

"You're fun, neighbor," she said. She lit a menthol. "You're just like me. Fun and crazy and bad to the bone." She cracked the window to exhale her stream of smoke. "I killed a man, you know."

34

Rook knew the Bronx from being tasked to the 4-1. Fort Apache was right, except the movie. It was always the cowboys against the Indians. The good guys against the bad. The movie wants to be socially something so you can get it that there's no black and white, somehow the good and the bad are connected, which is bullshit. Paul Newman was okay. Ed Asner should have Mumia raping him in the shower. Ken Wahl, good in the flick, great in *Wiseguy*, then he wrecks himself on his bike.

Lucas swung over to Betty's to get the milkshakes, but the place was gone. Grace wanted to go to the Fulton Fish Market where she could smell the ocean, which got him heading back home.

Her cell rang. She spoke for a minute and then covered the phone.

"Please say you won't be mad at me Lucas. Please, please."

"About what, Gracey?"

"Our dinner's cancelled."

He high-beamed the slow moving car in front of them. "That's okay," he told her. "I didn't know we were having it."

She finished her phone conversation and then turned to Rook.

"Judge Schwarzman is taking me someplace fancy. In his white stretch limo. Swans mate for life, you know. Isn't that yummy?"

"Just peachy, Grace. And yummy too."

When he pulled up to their building, Rook had the night man watch the Avanti while he took Grace upstairs.

"You're a peach," she said at her door.

Rook took the fiberglass coupe back to Rosen's, then stopped for a six pack to take back to his apartment. It would be good if the apartment was his. When it came time to put himself out to pasture, he could sell it and have some money so he could not give a fuck before his brain turned to mush like Tuze, or if he was lucky, he got to put a round in his head the day before.

He called Catherine Wren. "I'm just pulling off the Turnpike," he said.

"You're not," she said.

"I'm not."

"I appreciate that you have respect for me, Lucas. What I said. What I need."

"Of course I do. I've got an appointment with the psychologist tonight. I called to tell you that."

"I love you," she said.

"Me too," he told her.

Rook hung up and called Cholly the shrink. Maybe she was right. He broke Herbie Banks' nose just because. And he felt fine about it.

"I'm calling for that appointment," he said.

"Real or pretend?"

"Real, like I told you. You going to be in your pj's, Cholly?"

"Pretend. Come on over at eight. My last patient just cancelled."

"What's your rate?"

"We'll talk about that too."

Lucas finished his Yuengling and stretched out on the sofa. He has another one, maybe that's good, it loosens him up.

Cholly Hepburn was alright. They had worked on this bestiality case is how they met. Michaels, the guy's name was, grabbing little dogs and kissing their private parts. Cholly was a fact witness, not a shrink, which meant that he didn't talk crazy shit and it turned out he liked guns. They hung a couple of times and got shit-faced once when Lucas told him about his dreams about his brother which Cholly didn't give him any mumbo jumbo about. Maybe in four or five years they talked a couple of more times, once on a case where Cholly the shrink was offering his professional testimony, so it was going to be alright that he talk to him now.

Cholly Hepburn had his office a half a block from Central Park. Civilians thought the park was beautiful, which it was until the sun went down unless you were into a hairy blowjob in the bushes. Or you're some defenseless jogger, who according to Fat Al Sharpton with his processed hair, enticed that pack of animals to tear her into pieces.

The shrink answered the door in a black sweat suit and slippers and with a cigarette in the corner of his mouth.

"Some of my clients think I should not smoke in my own place. My office is in the front room, so it's a place of business." He lit the cigarette. "I say fuck 'em."

The office was small, three chairs, a picture on one wall of a door opening on to a lake.

"You want to, we can do this across the breakfast table. The rules are the same." He led Rook into his kitchen, which smelled like sauerkraut.

"What's the rules, Cholly?"

Hepburn held up four fingers. "There's three of them. First, you always tell me the truth. Second, you don't censor yourself. Last, you can quit whenever you want, except after you do, you have to come back once more. Except for tonight."

Rook sat down at the black and white enamel table.

"How's that?"

"Tonight doesn't count. That's why I said we'll talk about my fees. This may not work out. We know each other already. I saw you throw up once."

"That was you, Cholly."

"Right, right." He took a deep drag on his Lucky and under-handed it into the sink. "So what do we got here, my friend?"

"I came home with blood on my shoe. My old lady doesn't like it."

"So you're here because of her?"

"Right."

"What about you?"

"I'm good," said Lucas.

"You got shot."

"I'm still here. He's not, Chol."

The shrink got up. "Post Traumatic Stress Disorder is real."

"All cops work the street got that."

"Bad dreams, muscle pain, lethargy, panic attacks. You want to talk about any of that while you're here, I'm making coffee."

"I'm good."

"The coffee's not. It's instant, which I have to admit I'm addicted to. I got real cream though."

"Black's good."

Cholly turned on the tea kettle. "Used to make this with an electric thingamabob you put in the coffee cup, heats the water right up. You still got those dreams you told me about that fine evening when one of us puked, we can talk about them or anything else. We got time."

He made the coffee and handed Rook a cup.

"I saw stuff on the street that was pretty rough. A guy cut in half, a dead kid. It's lousy shit. It's got to brother you."

The shrink lit another smoke. "You said *brother*."

"I meant to say *bother*. This gives you a key to unlock my head?"

"Nope. Your twin brother got killed, right? It can't be any uglier than that."

"I saw it. I took care of it." He sipped his coffee. "Worse than station house brew, doc."

"Taking care of it, that enough for you?"

Lucas picked his cup up again and put it down.

"You're busting my stones here, Chol?"

"You're looking for answers, I can help you find them." He lit another Lucky.

Rook got up. "I'm good. And I appreciate your seeing me. If Catherine calls, let her know I was here."

"Can't do. It's against our ethics rules."

"What I owe you, doc?"

"Twenty bucks. I'm not charging you, but this can't be for free either. You come back, it'll be a hundred." He inhaled the cigarette smoke deeply. "Let me get you a receipt. You can show that to your friend. I'll leave the amount out. You know, 'One session, paid in full.' "

Lucas handed him the cash. "And I don't want anything in writing I was here."

They shook hands and the shrink held up the receipt.

"You can redeem it for a fabulous gift."

"I'm supposed to ask you what that is, Chol, I'm not."

"You're not *supposed* to do anything. And I'm just being a pain in the ass." Dr. Hepburn looked at his watch. "Which I'm going to do for the next seventeen minutes because you're my patient here. You paid for it."

Rook looked at his watch.

"The fabulous free gift is this," said the shrink. "Your brother's dead. Bad things happen to people we love. That's something we can't do anything about. But the people who killed him are dead. The man who tried to kill you is dead. Your neighbor who saved you, I heard on the tube she's going to be okay. It's all over, all that blood. Except maybe a drop on your shoe."

"I get that."

"And the part about you, Lucas. You're redeemed too. Redeemed, free, liberated, delivered. Here's your golden ticket." He handed over the receipt.

"That's a lot of words, Cholly. Which is when I head out of here."

"You don't get that? You don't get the part about you?"

"See you, Chol."

The shrink snubbed out his smoke. "I'm talking to you as our friend here. The way you're living your life, it means a hard way for the bad guys, Lucas Rook, but for you too. I want you to think about that."

Rook called Catherine Wren on the way downtown.

"I'm on the Turnpike. One exit away."

"No, you're not."

"I saw the shrink, Cat. I got a receipt to prove it. It went very well."

" 'Very well'? That doesn't sound like you."

"His words. I'll tell you all about it over some good Italian food."

"I've got exams to grade. Besides, it's too late."

"He told me to share, Catherine. I'll bring a tomato pie."

"One visit doesn't…"

"Pizza and a beer. It gets me that."

"Okay," she said. "I'll see you soon."

"In about an hour and a half, Cat. You can get some work done."

Rook went to his apartment, showered and changed. Then he went to Rosen's garage to get his Mercury. He took the back way to the garage. Maybe that's asking for it if you didn't know the alley like he did, where the light was, the hiding places. The row of trashcans, the dumpsters.

Lucas was almost through when the unmarked pulled in. Antopol opened his window.

"Good, good," said the detective. "I got another piece for you. And maybe you got my money a couple of hours early."

Antopol took a folder off the passenger's seat and opened his door. "You'll cream your jeans what I have here on Dwight Graves."

He got out of his unit with the folder in his left hand. Three shots. Different weapons. Two hit Rook in the Kevlar vest he was still too paranoid to take off. The other hit Antopol in the side of his head.

Lieutenant Jaluski walked in with his service weapon in his hand. Lucas Rook was sitting against a green dumpster. He tossed his ankle rig and stuck his back-up piece in the sleeve of his jacket.

"A regular thing with you, Rook, getting shot," said Jaluski. He checked on Antopol. "Poor Stanley. He just couldn't get it out of his head that you fucked up his life having him working Department files for you."

"I wonder who gave him that idea," said Rook.

"He was a bad cop, I caught him."

Lieutenant Jaluski took a pen out of his pocket and picked up Antopol's weapon by the trigger guard. "I guess I should have yours too," he said. "Securing the scene the way I am. And for which you should be thanking me for saving your sorry ass." He took Rook's .45.

"I'll send you a Hallmark card with kittens on it. That do it, Lieutenant?"

"You got a big mouth."

"You need somebody to follow your old lady? Maybe peek through some windows?" Lucas said.

Jaluski came in close. "You're a troublemaker just like your brother, which is what got him what he got."

"So you're not calling the meat wagon for me, I owe you big time, right, Lieutenant?"

"Everybody knows you're nuts, Lucas Rook. So whatever you say, with that big mouth of yours. Whatever you say." He had Antopol's gun in his right hand.

Rook slid his back-up piece down his sleeve and shot Jaluski through the throat. "How about I say 'paid in full,' you rat fuck. How about that?"

Lucas put his ankle rig on and went back through the alley and the long way around to Sid Rosen's. He gave Sidney his gun to get rid of with the garage's automotive shit and then went out to see Catherine Wren.

Rook called Cholly the shrink from her favorite pizzeria where he waited for the veggie special and the pepperoni on the side.

"Chol, about what you said for me to think about, how it's fucked up for me and the bad guys, the way I am. Well, you're right. At least about half of it you are."

END

Coming soon, the next Lucas Rook mystery:

BROKEN NIGHT